Waiting
to be.
written

By J. P. Legaspi

Book graphic project by Natalia Junqueira (Dawn Book Design)

ISBN: 978-1-7364110-0-1

US Copyright: TXu 2-228-614

FIRST EDITION

For all true love stories, from Romeo and Juliet to Ben and Ida (*Waiting to be Written*), from Marko and Alana (*Saga*) to Jack and Sally (*A Nightmare before Christmas*), and from Noah and Allie (*The notebook*) to You and Yours, there's perfection in the chaos and breathlessness in its complexity. Simple is the story and memorable are the details. Thanks to all the 'How we met' and 'Our story' accounts, both fictional and personal, that have shaped this book and warmed my heart. Special thanks to all those who supported me in this venture furthered me along this path. My gratitude is never ending as I hope your story is as well.

Contents

Chapter One

There are few truly magical moments in one's life. Even rarer still, an intertwined magical moment in two people's lives, such as on one Friday afternoon, when Idalis and Ben locked eyes for the first time, preceded by an unassuming accidental touch. The two strangers, and soon would-be lovers, reached for the same publication at the same time. Each withdrew in apology and then stood frozen, helpless victims of infatuation at first sight. As we all know, infatuation really is the seed for love. If tended properly and nourished with a tender heart, love can grow despite any obstacles.

The publication in question was Issue #1 of the epic space opera/fantasy graphic novel series *Saga*, written by Brian K. Vaughan and illustrated by Fiona Staples, published by Image Comics. Like Alana and Marko, the central characters, the attraction between Idalis and Ben was undeniable. But as the book unfolds, we find the path to a blissful union is not an easy one. Nevertheless, when the heart speaks, one must, at the very least, listen.

The silence in that timeless exchange of glances must be doubly appreciated in the backdrop of, arguably, one of the most sensory overloaded environments man has ever created: the New York Comic Convention. When their hands touched, their eyes met, and their skipped heartbeats gave reason to pause, as everything else in that maelstrom of controlled chaos faded into the background.

For those who have never had the pleasure to experience NYC Comic Con, imagine yourself in the middle of an indoor carnival, or maybe a casino, and then multiply stimuli and commotion by ten. It's like multiple airplane hangars converged into one futuristic, inter-galactic space station, then subdivided into villages. Hanging from every conceivable rod, beam, and rafter are endless posters, displays, and LED light signs as big as houses. Most setup consists of cleverly crafted gigantic exhibitions ranging from comic book icons like The Incredible Hulk to a re-created stage set of AMC's *The Walking Dead*. It has the feel of a slice of Hollywood.

The floor is further subdivided. The video gamers have a home here, complete with leather-seated consoles with the latest and greatest video games, usually with virtual reality as a featured prod-uct. In the center sits the mainstream publishing houses with mazes of cramped shelves of books, graphic novels, and comic books. All the production houses' setups promote the latest big-budget movie premieres. Then there are aisles of independent comic book market-ers, with their endless cardboard boxes filled with nearly every darn comic book ever made. People line up with agendas on hand, hunt-ing for prioritized items and diamonds in the rough.

And then there are those, like our lovestruck couple, who casu-ally finger through boxes, mostly aimlessly, until something extraor-dinary grabs hold of them, like a treasured rare issue or a personal connection to a character or plotline. And when something strikes their fancy, they gotta have it—or, in this case, get to know more about that other person.

All along the convention hall's perimeters are vendors peddling everything from cheap jewelry to expensive costumes to every kind of copyright-infringed fan art that exists! There are pins, cell phone holders, key chains, unicorns, knights, aliens, weapons, props, toys, collectables, stuffed animals, posters, more unicorns, more toys, and more everything. It is the fanboy or fangirl's wet dream come to fruition!

Throughout this magical land are lines, lines, and endless lines as far as one can see and then turn left. These circumvent in serpentine folds, mostly leading to the big name vendors like the Funko Pops stand, where people wait an hour for their favorite cartoon toy likeness, like the iconic horror/thriller film director Alfred Hitchcock, or the legendary Marvel comic book creator Stan Lee, or, heck, even Dr. Frankenstein's monster. But that doesn't hold a candle to the two- or three-hour wait for an autographed copy of anything by a celebrity artist, creator, or personality.

Lines at amusement parks in summer seem shorter in comparison. These adoring fans will patiently drain their phone's batteries as they inch their way toward that ten-second (if that) meet and greet. Some of these revered personalities are gregarious, cordial, and approachable. Some are stately, disconnected, and a tad snobbish. A few wouldn't make eye contact if you were the Messiah with an iridescent glow, sporting a sun-beamed halo drenched in a Technicolor dreamcoat!

Spots of the mini-city blare with electronic pulsating beats, but it's mostly muted by the murmur of thousands of conversations clamoring throughout the cavernous halls. And that's just it: the people at the convention are the real story. The majority are dressed up in costume, imitating a character from a movie, book, or video game. A costume is what the casual trick or treater will wear for Halloween, but cosplay is serious. It is costume-wearing on another level, embodying the character, not just the outfit, but the whole persona!

What a sight to behold, and even better to partake in. At least two-thirds of the hundreds of thousands of milling patrons were disguised in full spirit of cosplay. This wide range varies from video game characters, to movie characters, to comic book heroes and heroines, to political and satirical figures, to anime characters—and just about anything in between. Many costumes are expensive and professionally crafted. Others are clearly homemade, with impressive, refined details, rivaling movie wardrobes. Fellow cosplayers often stop and request photos with each other. It's an opportunity to express one's fantasies and just freaking have fun! The inner child is allowed to run free! Live on, Comic Con!

But back to our would-be lovers.

In delayed embarrassment, Ben withdrew his hand quickly and mustered a few words. "I'm so sorry. I just…"

Ben, or, more precisely, Benito Emilio Williams, was dressed up as Akecheta, a fictitious Native American character from the HBO series *Westworld* (based on the 1973 film of the same name, written and directed by Michael Crichton). He wore a pitch black, wavy hairpiece. The top of his head was crowned by a bun, and the rest of the hair flowed down the sides of his cheeks and behind his head. The upper half of his face was painted in slick, glossy black, and the lower half was a crusty, volcanic white.

Ida was further captivated by his melting light hazel eyes, bookended by his well-defined cheekbones and full lips. His jawline had red handprints that stood out against the white background, and the rest of his bare-chested body was layered in the same crusty white body paint. And, like his face paint, this could not hide his chiseled, lean, muscular frame. A few faintly noticeable tattoos added to his allure. Tight black leather pants outlined an athletic pair of sturdy quads. Not much was left to the imagination. As a member of the fictitious Ghost Nation tribe, he was an outstanding reproduction. If he were a stripper, he'd cash in a fortune tonight.

Ben continued to fumble his words. "Ah… I… The thing is…"

Ida, or, more precisely, Idalis Charmaine Shah, was dressed as Gamora, a comic book character appearing in American comic books published by Marvel Comics, created by writer/artist Jim Starlin. Gamora belongs to an elite intergalactic force made popular by the 2014 movie *Guardians of the Galaxy*. Ida's costume was more of a loose interpretation. She was donning a revealing black leather vest and tight leather purplish pants. The vest seemed to stretch beyond its capacity, and her well-endowed chest bulged from its restraints. Her long, straight black hair was highlighted three-quarters of the way down in light fuchsia, complementing her pants nicely. All of her exposed skin was covered in green body paint. Knee-high black leather boots completed her outfit, elevating her look from stunning to *goddamn*.

It was incredibly challenging for Ben to not stare at her well-proportioned curves, her body-hugging costume, and her gorgeous face. Everything moved in a sleek, smooth switch. Her coke-bottle shape was jaw-dropping. Gamoras were a dime a dozen today, but no one else rocked this character like she did. Her beauty was indisputable. Her eyes captivated with their expressive deep brown color, thick black outline, and sensual almond shape. Those eyes couldn't lie if they tried. Her eyebrows were expertly tweezed, and her eyelashes were as long and curved as she was. When she spoke, her perfectly articulated British accent sharpened the words that echoed from full, sensual lips. That voice was sweet yet affirmative, furthering Ben's descent. Her long, slender face, with its high cheekbones and radiant smile, hinted at mixed features similar to his own diverse heritage. It highlighted the uniqueness at the heart of her stunning beauty.

Ben's inner voice chastised him, finally bringing him to a somewhat conscious state. Subtly, he pinched his own thigh, swallowed a cleansing gulp of nervousness, and tried to speak, but still, only an empty semblance of sound was uttered: "Ah…"

Ida crested her melting smile and replied, "No worries. I believe that treasured item caught a glimpse of us both. We reached it simultaneously, however, I concede it to you, proud warrior." Ida was also taken by Ben and had shocked herself by being uncharacteristically coy. She blinked furiously and bashfully in a flirtatious, submissive way, clearly overplaying the docile role, then scanned the floor vacantly. This was most unlike her, as you will come to know, but most endearing to Ben.

He finally spoke up, cracking in a soprano tone and then deepening it, defenselessly overcompensating. Then he erupted into informative speed babble, not taking one breath: "*Saga* Issue #1, where we are introduced to Alana and Marko's story line from the perspective of their kid, an unexpected child from two warring races. It's one of the more recent masterpiece sagas of love during intergalactic wartime."

Ida's eyes locked into his and she added, "It's an enduring love story, where they literally have to fight every possible obstacle to survive, as everything and everybody tries their darndest to tear them apart. It's dreadfully addictive!"

"It's a beautiful and poetic tale against all the odds!" agreed Ben.

"It's what true love is all about," finished Ida.

Again, silence filled the void of their immediate surroundings as the sparks flew.

Ben snapped out of his trance and offered, "Look, please, you take it. I insist. I have a mint copy already. This one is signed, but big whoop! I'd rather another true, avid fan have it."

"Oh, I absolutely could not and would not. That is most kind of you, and very chivalrous, but I'll have to insist. Besides, I'm certain you placed your hand on it first. In my haste I must have knifed in and jabbed my battle-hardened tentacles on it. Please, I was merely going to peruse the collection. I have the entire series, and I do adore it so. All my collectibles are in storage, in England. What's more, I'm not into signed copies. Just a fan of the story, any really well-told story."

"England?" an even-more-intrigued Ben asked.

"Naturally. You think this charming accent was perfected in some basement in Spokane?"

Ben was flabbergasted, rendered speechless, and blushing under his crusty white face paint. He pressed himself to say something, but the mechanics of articulation were reduced to a few flattering laughs.

"But don't fret, you chaps in the States have much more fun!"

Ben eased into a smile, grateful that Ida had filled in the potential conversation-killer of dead air and hadn't politely excused herself yet. He finally returned, "I think you'd be devastatingly charming in any language. French, Spanish, Mandarin… heck, even sign language."

Now it was Ida's turn to blush, albeit similarly hidden underneath her own green makeup. However, the quick-witted fangirl surprised Ben by waving her middle fingers at the ceiling and declaring, "So, you find this incredibly charming, do you? Well, as the daughter or Thanos and the harbinger of his of callous thinning of the universe, I shall rain down upon thee a furious wrath, the likes of which you've never seen before, mere human!"

Not to be outdone, Ben grabbed at his crotch and raised his voice, spewing contempt and flares of rage. "Screw this world and all the big business conglomerates! Down with the oppressors and exploiter scum!"

Ida nodded with appreciation and growing infatuation. She joined him in vulgarity and random protest until an enormous, burly security guard approached. He was not amused, steaming toward the two with pressed lips and pinched eyebrows. He addressed them in a smoky, deep, scratchy, and commanding voice: "I'm going to ask you clowns to leave if you keep this horseshit up!"

Ben apologized immediately. He feared losing the moment with this ultra-attractive Gamora. "Sir, please, we were just—"

"Just getting into character, good sir," explained the dramatic Ida. "We surely did not want to cause a scene or offend anyone, much less make spectacles of ourselves at this venue of free expression. After all, we're savage outlaws, good kind officer!" she added with an overemphasized batting of eyelids and a most seductive smile.

She nudged Ben's ribs in a most disarming manner and winked. The imposing patrolman had been smoldering, but now he rolled his eyes, sighed, and warned, "Tone it down, or you'll be making asses of yourselves on the street." He made a thumbing gesture toward the exit doors. He had deescalated his tone toward Ida but looked back at Ben with a reprehensible intensity and smirky disdain. Upon leaving, he deliberately leveled a stern forearm shiver into Ben's right shoulder, nearly knocking him to the ground.

Ben's eyes trailed the guard with contentment. Normally, the mild-mannered Ben would take issue with the unnecessary physicality, but he was in the presence of someone very captivating. In an instant, his mesmerized eyes returned to Ida, lovestruck.

But Ida took exception. "Hey! Now that was absolutely uncalled for, officer!" Her words fell on deaf ears. She returned to Ben. "Are you all right?

He searched for words that just wouldn't materialize, then nodded. His scowl at the security guard faded.

Then, curiously, Ida erupted into hysterical laughter, and Ben's gifted power of speech returned. "That was simply amazing! Real quick thinking!"

"What was amazing?" She cocked her head back and let out a high-pitched guffaw. "Sweetheart, you of all people should know. You men are so predictably shameless! All one has to do is appeal to your ego, and all the other parts that go along with it, both large and small, and you are putty, simply putty in our hands."

Ben paused, and then agreed. "Well, I guess, guilty as charged, all the large and less large parts of me."

Ida nodded at his subtle wit and returned with but a smile, "Touché."

Ben replied, *"Mademoiselle, je vous assure, coupable comme accusé."*

"Tres bon," replied a stunned Ida. Few things drew her attention like a quick wit. In the ensuing silence, butterflies fluttered about. These two were sizing up each other and this sudden piqued curiosity. They were processing the person before them and where to go from here. Breathing typically stops at this moment, as thoughts are overrun by emotions.

Ida noticed a marred spot on Ben's shoulder paint, where the wannabe lawman had flexed his authoritative dominance, exposing Ben's copper-toned skin and lean, muscular shoulder. Ida declared, "Oh, my! That swine brute ruined your war paint!"

She reached for his shoulder, breaking Ben's hypnotized gaze. He inspected the discontinuity of his body paint, flexing his deltoids and bicep in doing so. Ida took notice. Her fingers caressed his shoulder. Her exquisitely manicured fingernails skimmed his skin like smooth pearls. Tactfully, Ida leaned back, panning his entire bare chest while Ben grimaced at the blemish. He felt aware of his chiseled frame and his fit physique. She raised her eyebrow at the imagination of what the rest of him would look like without the cosmetics—or the clothing.

Exhaling subtly, she complimented, "Wow, that really is an exquisite ensemble you have on, I must say! It is quite the shame he ruined all your hard work."

Ben replied in agreement, silently thankful the mark gave Ida the opportunity to touch his skin. Her gentle caress shot electric bolts through his nerves and down into his loins. His eyes sank in weakened surrender, as his sudden arousal would soon be noticeable in his already-stretched leather pants.

She paused for a moment, then edged her fingers down his well-toned arms and intertwined her fingers with his. She seemed to be a master at disarming men, and Ben was at her mercy. His grip was flaccid at best, but it was the only thing flaccid about him. Her initially gentle grasp suddenly strengthened into a firm clutch. She scanned the maze that is the Comic Con landscape, then drew his hand up, pulled him toward her, and enthusiastically cried, "Come with me!"

Ben's normally apprehensive and skeptical default response was nowhere to be found. He was blissfully powerless in her hands. His overcautiousness took a back seat, and he allowed himself to be led. Something about her freed him from his own limitations as he eagerly allowed himself to be whisked away.

He was absolutely, unequivocally, and ecstatically hers.

Chapter Two

Ida haphazardly led the charge through the multitude of costumed visitors, with frequent pauses, redirections, and vigorous sprints. Ben normally would have grown frustrated by now and abandoned the trek altogether, but this was the most excited he had been for some time. This stunning, gorgeous person had captivated his heart as she advanced them through the large fantasy marketplace. Burning hot blood rushed through his veins. Not long ago, he'd considered skipping the convention altogether. Now he deemed himself the luckiest person ever to be there.

She, too, was in uncharted waters. Ida's life was scheduled and regimented, rooted in purpose and measured by how many things she'd crossed off her to-do list. She had been molded into a workaholic on the fast track up the corporate ladder, but her true self was more carefree and adventurous. The thrill of the mission at hand catered to her sense of duty and problem-solving, although these were fading thrills. Somewhere along the way, she had veered toward the Puritan work ethic at the expense of diminishing self-satisfaction. Today had cracked the window of her mundanity, providing a welcomed fresh air of release.

Finally, she halted to a stop, with Ben nearly crashing into her from behind. She exclaimed, "I knew I saw it earlier! Behold, salvation!"

Ben took a moment to get his bearings, then realized they were standing in front of a cosplay first aid station. Here, a vast array of tapes, glues, and sewing kits were made available for those who had suffered costume defect or malfunction. The consideration of mending his swiped patch of makeup was heartwarming and thoughtful. It was the last thing he had expected. He thought she was surely leading him to some hidden gem booth or a *Saga*-related item. Now they were there for him.

Ben smiled at Ida with deep gratitude and an unmistakable pinch of coquetry. As he engaged the staff about the type of aid that would blend his white makeup smear, Ida took the opportunity to observe Ben's interaction, his animated body language, his sincere smiles, and his free-flowing social self. He had instantly charmed the two female workers. She considered herself quite progressive but thought there was nothing wrong with appreciating Ben's manly mannerisms and his soft-spoken tone. *Quite a rare blend,* she thought. He was not a charmer; he was being himself, naturally likeable. She was turned on.

It was a liberating feeling for her. In the business world, where she spent most of her life, she had to build a certain image, an image that she felt wasn't totally representative of her true self. That image was cutthroat and vicious, a rigid hardliner and unpliable negotiator. How could she not be drawn to Ben? But her inner voice demanded she stop this at once. She was not mentally or spiritually ready to open herself up to anyone, much less someone she met at a comic book convention.

This is crazy, she chastised herself while maintaining her smile, clenching her teeth.

Ben's costume was remedied, and he proudly proclaimed, "Wow, look, good as new!" He modeled his restored scuff patch, and Ida observed with unrestrained appreciation. Completely mended, he looked absolutely appetizing.

She bit her lower lip and agreed. "Smashing success, indeed. You're terribly symmetrical in every way! All prim and proper to slay the colonial invaders."

Ida cringed inside while maintaining her smile. Had she actually uttered those words? She was in a whole new realm, reacting uncharacteristically, admiring Ben's physique and buckling at his personality. Her drive for career success condemned such conduct, though it was shamelessly touted by the misogynistic old boys' club. Why was she now overwhelmed so primally?

Never one to live in denial, she knew the answer. Ida hadn't been this physically attracted to someone in a long time, and it had been even longer since she was involved in any romantic relationship. Ben's total persona, with his easy, infectious personality and straight-up warrior ensemble, had hooked her, plain and simple. She gazed upon Ben, whose words fell on deaf, defenseless, wonderstruck ears.

Ben seemed relaxed and less anxious. "Hey, again, I'm blown away that you thought of this. It's super cool of you to get me all fixed up. I didn't even know these booths existed!"

Ida was still in a cloudy daydream, and she acknowledged her aloofness. "Apologies," she said. "All this noise can be a bit much."

Ben repeated, even more adorably than before, "You're very cool to get me patched up. That guy was a real prick. You're very thoughtful."

"Oh, poppycock! There's no need for that, honestly. You're right as rain now. That's all that matters." She took a deep breath, bobbing her head mechanically.

"Poppycock?" Ben was amused. "That's a great word."

Ida again grew flushed from the flattery. She felt like a timid young lady, unsure exactly how to respond.

"So, why Gamora?" asked Ben.

She appreciated that the question gave her pause, let her catch a breath and refocus. "Well, she's a decisive person who, despite sordid beginnings, knows right from wrong and is intent on carving her own path, adapting along the way. But moreover, she's a complete badass!"

Ben fumbled over his words. "You are. Ah, I mean, Gamora is. And you definitely probably are as well."

She took a mocking stance of insult before asserting, "Isn't it obvious?"

A shared lighthearted laugh undercut the ten-mile-thick tension.

Now it was Ida's turn to ask. "And your choice?"

She tried not to completely melt as Ben smiled and then explained like a delighted child on Halloween, "They were all out of extra-large SpongeBobs, so it was either this or Buzz Lightyear. And since I already dress up as Buzz for one of my part-time gigs—"

"One of many part-time gigs?"

Ben's panic raged like a five-alarm fire, and he quickly sought to remedy it. "I do have a few things going on, but I've made most, if not all, of my credit card payments last month and my parents haven't kicked me out yet."

"I see," said Ida, with a skeptical arch of her eyebrow.

"I'm kidding, of course. I have my own place, with a roommate, and I don't have creditors hunting me down. I pay my rent on time. I am employed, but I am not my job. I am, in my heart of hearts, an aspiring writer, and all my other gigs keep the lights on. Someday, I will make it as a published author."

The ensuing silence paralyzed Ben's entire body. All his insecurities were knocking as one on his stopped heart. He froze, breathless with puppy dog eyes, in anticipation of a hasty exit by the piercing Gamora. Every second that elapsed drove the dagger of rejection deeper and deeper into his core.

Then Ida turned her head sideways and studied Ben. She was hard to read, torturing Ben with every gaze. She finally asked, "A writer, huh? Writing what? And don't for the love of bangers and mash say, 'Roses are red'!"

Relieved, Ben felt air reenter his lungs. He held his palms up, asking for her consideration. "Hold on! I can show you!" He dropped to one knee, and dropped his messenger bag and nervously struggled with the zippers until hastily spilling its contents all over the convention floor. Lip balm, cough drops, eye drops, candy wrappers, pens, pencils, phone charger cords, a phone battery, Post-its, paper receipts, comic books, pins, magnets, handouts, business cards, and Band-Aids littered their feet.

"Blimey! This is worse than me grandma's purse, and hers has wheels on it!"

Oblivious to the clutter, Ben targeted a single marble notebook and retrieved it with glorious elation before handing it to Ida. "I've been writing all my life without really knowing what I want to write about. Full disclosure: I love horror, and wicked thoughts, and dark humor. But I'm not a dark person. I don't have black everything or dress like Dracula's minion. I also have a weak spot for action, obviously, comics and fantasy and sci-fi. But one day it hit me in some weird, alternate-universe epiphany." Ben extended his hand, offering the notebook to Ida. "This is the beginning of my very incomplete life's work, still waiting to be written."

Ida stared at the notebook, overwhelmed. It was not often a complete stranger impressed her to this extent. But this man and his notebook had done it. As she cautiously reached out and placed her hand on the notebook, she raised her eyes to meet Ben's and quipped, "This is your masterpiece?"

Ben hesitated, steadying his breath, and then exhaled, "Yes."

Her stare returned to the notebook as she read the inscription out loud. *"Waiting to be Written,* by Benito Emilio Williams." Her eyes darted back up to Ben's, placing a full name to this handsome, proud, Native American warrior. She said, "Pleasure to meet you, Benito."

"Ben, please."

Ida smiled as only her natural radiance allowed, then curled her free hand toward herself. "Idalis."

Ben reached out with his free hand and took hers in a gentle handshake. "Nice to meet you, Idalis."

"Ida, please."

"Ida it is."

Ida tugged at the notebook, but Ben held firm, drawing an inquisitive look. Ben explained, "There are loads of spelling, grammar, and syntax errors, but no errors in content or intent. I just write so fast, but not as fast as I think. There is a direction, maybe several, and tons of material and characters and random thoughts. I got so many well-developed characters and subplots somehow interwoven. I even have a kick-ass ending, but the middle…"

Ida maintained eye contact as she inched her fingers to his. She drew him in toward her and whispered softly in his ear, "I'm honored you would show me this and entrust a perfect stranger. Rest assured; I love a good story."

With that, she slowly released his grip on the notebook by lifting each finger individually. Then she placed her hand on the left side of his firm chest and reassured, "Don't worry so much. Thank you. And I won't make or break you, I can tell. You will follow your dreams regardless."

The words were magical, almost therapeutic. He was unsure what to do as Ida began to read. Her facial expressions morphed from confused to intrigued to delighted, then back to confused. At times she laughed. At one point her eyes even began to water. But she held her composure and continued reading. All along, Ben's gut twisted and turned and knotted up like a schoolboy having his paper reviewed by the principal. Despite his trepidation, an inner voice calmed him as he patiently watched her read. He couldn't look away from her dazzling expressions and her easing fingers on his chest. He thought that even her most contorted looks were so damn sensual.

She had managed to read intensely and uninterrupted through twelve pages. Then she saw a stunningly gorgeous man dressed as Sunny from the AMC television series *Into the Badlands*. The outfit was incredibly accurate, its red leather sheen slick and eye-catching. His costume outlined a fit and strapping athletic build. This taller, more strikingly handsome regent (a bodyguard, or a "clipper" as termed on the series), had that commanding look, serious and confident and, yeah, cocky.

This Sunny slid behind Ida, wrapped his long fingers over her eyes, and jabbed, "I lost you once, and I couldn't bear to lose you again, my love! It would just kill me, absolutely tear me to shreds!" He spoke with a dry, raspy voice, almost overdone, and with a clearly possessive tone. Even fully heterosexual Ben had to acknowledge that this tall and debonair male before him was undeniably gorgeous. His heart sank like a ten-foot anchor in a thousand-mile-deep trench.

Ida swiped at his hands and cursed, "Damn you, Kurt!"

Sunny retorted, now in a high-pitched, smoother voice, "So, you don't believe in answering your phone? How in the hell would I find you in this moose crossing people fest!" He turned his disapproving peepers at Ben and said, "And who the hell are you?" He lowered his eyes, aiming his interrogation right through Ben's soul.

Ben was caught between worlds, completely flummoxed. A few seconds ago, he was in a happily preoccupied state of wonder. A woman carved out of his idealized dreams, in personality and form, had taken an interest in his most cherished passion. Ben was not one to post his writing online. He had never allowed anyone to read it, much less critique it. For him, this was as personal as it could get. He had scribbled discontinuous side notes, catch phrases, and poetic stanzas in the margins. The notebook also contained the occasional personal entry. Every now and then a song title was scribbled in, with reminders of the feeling and inspiration it brought. This was not only his narrative; it was his fragile soul in print.

He had freely and eagerly opened a window into his world. If she dropped the book and ran toward the burly security guard, so be it. It would have been a monumental blow, but he had to take the risk. If she genuinely embraced it, he would skyrocket into a new stratosphere.

Before Ben could respond, Ida punched Sunny in the arm and he winced like a schoolboy. Sunny returned a bevy of expletives that would have made the rough gangs he grew up with proud. Bed surmised that they were a couple. His dejection deepened.

Sunny declared, "You know what's up! And we're moving along!" The two were deadlocked in an overexaggerated stare down. For Ben, it lasted a tormenting lifetime. It looked like neither would yield. Security might have been alerted. Her fists were clenched, and smoke seemed to billow from his nostrils. Then, without any warning, Ida softened her stance and slowly relaxed. She wiggled her fingers loose, shrugged her shoulders, and spoke in a robotic tone, further perplexing Ben:

"Ben, this is Kurt, dressed up as Sunny. Kurt, this is Ben, dressed up as Akecheta."

The men exchanged awkward nods. Neither offered a gentle-manly handshake. Ben gathered himself in the now-very-uncom-fortable moment and began to speak, but he was immediately cut off.

"I can't wait to read the finished product...." Ida trailed off, then abruptly closed the notebook and handed it back to a stunned Ben, whose mouth was agape. Ida sucked in her lower lip and fluttered her eyelids, not in a flirtatious manner, but a conflicted one. As she turned away, she muttered a barely audible, "Good luck. I like it a lot."

In a quicker time than he could register, she vanished amongst the sea of people, the writhing ocean of everything dazzling and blinding. Ben stood like a statue, holding his notebook, struggling to not crumble into a thousand pieces.

Chapter Three

Ida stomped and marched like a threatened rhino, bumping into unsuspecting convention-goers and bulldozing displays and just about anything else that stood in her way. Kurt trailed her stride by stride for as long as he could, until the crisscross of the masses and some dead stops stalled his pursuit. Finally, they arrived at the gender neutral/family/for everyone bathroom. She zipped straight to the head of the line and grabbed the door as someone exited. The line volleyed a tumultuous cascade of irate curses at her!

"Apologies! I have a medical condition!" screamed Ida as she bolted into the restroom. She flung Kurt inside, followed him in, locked the door, then apologized again before unleashing her own fury of unintelligible profanity. All the while, loud bangs pounded away at the door.

After her tirade had faded to a slow simmer, Ida reached into her purse and grabbed a fistful of dollars. She quickly unlocked the door, flung the cash at the crowd, then just as quickly slammed the door shut and relocked it. For the time being, the people in line were tamed.

Inside the restroom, Ida tore into Kurt. "What the hell, Kurt!"

"What the hell with you! Listen, girlfriend, it's one thing to play the unsavory role of your cockblocking, overprotective, bitch-ass boyfriend, but it is absofreakinlutely another thing to be treated like one! Okay? So cool your jets, missy! You are not wiping the blade of your a-hole ex on my back! Holy heck no!"

Ida remained quiet but smoldering, like the Krakatoa eruption of 1883. Kurt continued, "Listen, I know you're in a tough spot with the whole Spencer thing. But you gotta let it go. Vanquish that blemish from your résumé. Move on, girl. That pretty, strapping Ghost Nation warrior would be a good start."

Ida wanted to form words, but she couldn't. She just dove into Kurt's chest and started to cry hysterically. Kurt wrapped his arms around her and consoled, "Let it out, girl. Let it out."

Just then, the intense hammering and hateful cursing returned. Kurt kicked the door and cried, "One minute, you degenerates!"

He turned back to Ida. "Okay, we have to get out of this filthy piss-hole soon, mostly because I cannot take one more minute of this urban perfume. Also, there isn't a cosplay first responder out there who can fix the hot mess you're making of my impeccable outfit!" With that, he separated himself, then studied her for a second and said, "You got a little... Hold up... Wait..."

"What!" asked Ida.

He grabbed a piece of tissue paper, wiped Gamora's eyelids, and then said, "Oh, how cute! You got a little sparkle in your eye for that barbarian, don't you? Oh, isn't that just precious."

"A sparkle? What are you, in grade school?"

"Call it what you want, dear, but when someone catches your eye, they catch your eye. Who is that delicious little thing?"

"Nobody!" exclaimed Ida. "I just met him."

"Well, that nobody twisted the woman of steel I once knew into a soft pretzel of love. And that's saying a lot, because you don't get impressed easily! You've got some lofty standards and odd, questionable taste."

"He's nobody, okay?"

"Please. Who the hell do you think you're talking to, sis?"

"Just drop it!"

"Oh, hell no. No!"

The intense banging was now accompanied by a security officer's vaguely familiar voice. "You guys who are in there, we heard that you cut the line! That's a big no-no!"

Kurt mocked him. "A big no-no!"

The reprimand continued, "There better not be any inappropriate behavior in there! That's a crime in this city!"

"This unhygienic latrine is the real crime!" returned Kurt.

"That's it, we're coming in and taking you out."

"Shit!" exclaimed Kurt. "Oh, great! Just freaking great. We're gonna get kicked out of Comic Con, and probably be blacklisted. So not how I envisioned upgrading my celebrity status. All for your 'Nobody.'"

Ida was quietly plotting an escape. "Quick! Let me see your snack bag."

"What snack bag?" replied Kurt with defensive eyes.

"Come on, I know you have an absolutely horrible addiction to all things unwholesome, and frankly it pisses me off to high heaven that you stay so fit and trim!"

"Don't hate, okay? It's very unbecoming."

Ida snarled, then grabbed Kurt's man bag and withdrew a Ziploc containing an assortment of chocolates, gummy bears, chips, cookies, Sour Patches, and the like. She formed a most wicked, sinister smile and chirped, "Don't worry, I'll replenish your stash. But right now, it's a get-out-of-jail card."

Ida proceeded to open Kurt's precious sweets bag and stuffed everything she could into her mouth. Kurt gasped in abhorrence. Ida chewed with forced bites and contorted facial expressions. She paused a few times to breathe, then forged on.

A different, deeper, and more menacing voice resonated through the doors. "Stand back! We are coming in."

Kurt's eyes widened, first at the door, then at Ida, who was composed despite her mouth bulging to the point of near explosion. She calmed Kurt with open palms and reassuring nods. Kurt pieced it all together and blinked in agape realization. A rustling of keys was clanging on the metal doors, with mumbled cursing in the background. Ida nodded again, then rushed toward the door.

Just as it opened, she stopped on a dime and greeted the security guards with a spew of partially digested food. Under the guise of shock and awe, Kurt apologized to the crowd and plainly explained, "Ah, sorry, folks. The stomach bug is a real bitch!"

Ida formed some semblance of apology and patted the security guard on the shoulder as she walked past him. It was the very same security guard that had bumped Ben earlier—an ironic measure of revenge. Kurt assisted a seemingly weakened Ida as the two hurriedly hobbled around the corner. Safely out of the guards' sight, they dropped gear and hauled ass out of the Jacob K. Javits Center, bursting into triumphant laughter. The soiled security guard stood staring at the debris that now decorated his shirt and pants and face. He himself felt his lunch creep up, and eventually he blew chunks as well. The tense line of restroom patrons was rendered speechless.

After a few seconds of stunned disbelief, the next person in line, who was dressed as Mario from the video game of the same name, waved caution to the wind and dashed into the stall. Finally, relief!

Chapter Four

Ben arrived at his apartment deflated. He turned the key and opened the door with the energy of a dying battery. A small measure of relief echoed in his exhale as he tossed his keys in the bowl, eased off his messenger bag, and flung his jacket on the coat rack, missing the hook by a wide margin. He noticed not and cared not. He dragged himself zombie-like toward the refrigerator and opened the door. It wasn't a long trek, as the living room merged with the kitchen and a small dining area. Some say New York is the poster child of the open-floor concept.

In the fridge he found raggedy boxes of takeout Chinese, a few leftover tacos with their oils soaking through the paper wrappings, some bottles of no-frills beer, a soymilk container, a couple of condiments, and shadows of not much else. In half-hearted disgust, he nudged the door closed.

In even more sluggish steps, he headed for the frayed couch, where he plopped headfirst, despondent. His already-peeling face paint smeared onto the worn fabric. Truthfully, the white streaks blended with the mosaic of the classic furniture piece, which had probably witnessed six or seven presidents.

He had ignored more than twenty missed calls and countless text messages from friends trying to track him down at Comic Con, seeking an update on his whereabouts. The pile of notifications was not uncommon, as he had been known to vanish for stretches of time. "Moody" was the term mostly used to describe Ben. There's a fine line between true depression and reclusive "me time," and Ben tiptoes across it. When inspired, he can lose himself in an endeavor for days, even weeks. That level of focus can be self-damaging. Once, he was so absorbed in a college project, designing a tiny home, that he dropped sixteen pounds in one month, grew a beard, and missed out on a friend's eighteenth birthday party.

After Ida's heart-crushing departure, he had no appetite for nourishment. He stood in the spot where she'd abruptly left him for about thirty minutes, processing. Feeling numb and dejected, the convention lost its appeal, and he was no good for any other human interaction. If there were a hidey-hole nearby, he'd have fought and clawed his way in and sealed it with a ten-ton boulder. But for now, the cozy couch would have to do.

Never-ending questions swirled in his head like a really bad hangover. Who was that girl, Idalis? Ida, rather! Who had captured his heart, breathed life into his soul? Had he really just allowed some complete stranger to read his most precious thoughts, thoughts he was frightened to death to show another human? And who was that exceedingly handsome, intimidating man who'd unraveled his dreams with a few choice words? Friend? Brother? Boyfriend? Ex-boyfriend? Stalker? Serial killer?

His brain was a runaway train speeding in circles. Eventually, it would derail. He thought they had spoken to each other like long-term relationship partners: comfortably vulgar and combative. To the third-party observer, it sounded like bitter countries at the brink of war. But to the trained ear, it was mom and pop's mundane banter about picking up after themselves.

Ben couldn't wrap his mind around how such a relatively short encounter had affected him so much.

He vacillated about what it all meant. Did she *like him*, like him, or was she just being friendly? Was she making small talk, or was she into him? Did she really like what she'd read? Was she being politely short or unimpressed? He had to know.

The vortex of emotions was making him nauseous. But he made no mistake: she was smoking hot, and her image was burned into his soul. *This was surely a bizarre day*, he thought. Good thing he had nothing inside his stomach to violently project.

The door of his roommate, Norbert Wilder, affectionately known as "Buddy," creaked open. The sound was largely unnoticed by the preoccupied Ben. Buddy was not exactly wheelchair bound, but he found it infinitely easier to navigate with it than without it. He silently wheeled out into the living room and studied Ben on the couch. He parked himself near the moping lump and then whacked his cane on Ben's dangling leg.

Ben sat up quickly. "Hey, yo! What gives!"

"Thought I saw a fly."

"Must have been one heck of a fly!" exclaimed Ben. "Besides, it's like October. They're all pretty much dead by now."

"I see one that ain't. Well, maybe almost dead, by the looks of you," laughed Buddy.

Ben rolled his eyes and buried his head under a throw pillow. He certainly was in no mood to talk to anyone, especially Buddy. Buddy was a Korean War veteran, married three times and divorced three times. He had held nearly every odd job and lost them all. Now in his early eighties, Buddy was still as sharp as a Marine's hunting knife. Like Ben, Buddy was an avid comic book and toy collector. His many possessions were spread out among a storage unit, his closet, and his bedroom. At one point, Buddy had to have his right leg amputated due to the diabetes ravaging his blood vessels. He also had a multitude of other health issues, like chronic obstructive pulmonary disease, high blood pressure, and arthritis, as a direct result of a lifetime of smoking, reckless living, and multiple motorcycle accidents.

In one of Ben's prior side hustles, he was delivering packages and one of his regular deliveries was to Buddy's doorstep. Never one to pass up conversation, the two always ended up chatting up a storm. Sensing Ben's good nature and as realizing their mutual need for a roommate, the stars aligned, and they became cohabitants in this fairly spacious three-bedroom rent controlled apartment. The cost was minimal for Ben, but he was expected to keep the house tidy and in order. The last thing Buddy would allow was for some stranger, namely an appointed home aide, to come in snooping through all his stuff and treating him like an invalid. He resolved that he would go out like he lived: on his terms, in his house, and surrounded by people of his choosing.

His stonewashed jeans looked like they had mopped every oil change spot in the garage but had never seen the inside of a washing machine. His shirts were always black tees, always with some outrageous design or profane saying. At times he wore his favorite black hooded sweatshirt or his similarly stained denim jacket. Nearly every inch of his body was etched by tattoos, and even a few brands, except for his face, which only had half a dozen you could see when he wasn't wearing the leather hat that covered his bald head. A wavy gray-white beard fluffed all the way down to his rotund belly. Buddy was the epitome of a rough road rebel.

He plopped himself down in his favorite spot, a cozy, lived-in, tattered beige La-Z-Boy and said, "You know, you can fool some of the people some of the time, but you can't fool me none of the time. What's eatin ya, kid?"

All that emanated from beneath Ben's buried face was the incoherent murmur of a broken-hearted young man.

Buddy added, "Yup, I thought so! Who is she and what'd you do?"

Ben slowly turned over and looked at Buddy with fascination before finally asking, "How the heck did you know it's about a girl?"

Buddy smiled and proudly thumped his chest. "Come on, kid. Who do ya think you're talking to, huh? Now, my tummy's growling, so out with it!"

Ben shook his head, struggling to talk, then finally managed, "Okay, there I was at the Comic Con. I really didn't want to go, but you know, Meck and Arty kept bugging me. They got me the pass, and so I went."

Buddy interrupted, "Dressed as Tonto?"

"Tonto?" puzzled Ben.

"Yeah, you know, the Lone Ranger and his sidekick, the Indian guy, Tonto."

"Buddy. You can't say that today. The appropriate terminology is 'Native American,' and no, I'm not dressed as Tonto. I'm Akecheta, a character from the HBO series *Westworld*."

Buddy downplayed his befuddlement. "Potato, potato. Same freakin difference. Now, Akuna who?"

"Look, I'm dressed as a character on a hit series. I'm having a good time when I thought I wouldn't. I picked up a couple of *Punisher War Zone* issues, a classic Green Lantern one, and a Joker anthology. You know, I was enjoying the day. Though it was getting a bit crowded, and you know my thing with crowds."

"Okay already! My dinner ran off back to the fridge' cause it got so cold. Let's go! And your damn Tonto paint better come off that couch! It's vintage, ya know! A freaking classic."

"All right. Fine. There I was, at some comic book table, reaching for a signed *Saga* Issue #1. It probably would have been too rich for my blood, but, heck, it was worth a look-see. I really did want it. Then, it was as if God himself sent his most beautiful angel to touch my hand as we both reached for the comic book. There was this… this…this spark."

"A spark? Like you soiled yourself?" guessed Buddy.

"No, not like that," clarified Ben.

"Like when you cum?"

"Jeez, Buddy. No. I mean, I was ridiculously aroused. But this was different."

"Sure, it wasn't the carpet?" prodded Buddy. "I mean, those things cause a hell of a shock."

Ben rolled his eyes again and exhaled. "Forget it." He smothered his face in the pillow again.

Buddy sharply returned, "Oh, dry your eyes and powder your nose, Nancy! I mean, Christ almighty! You kids today are like damn fine china! Y'all should wear signs that read, 'Fragile, handle with care'!"

Ben remained unmoved, silent, and—if possible—more crest-fallen.

Buddy squinted sinisterly then teased, "Heck, she wasn't all that fine. What, was she dressed up like some alien chick or something? It's prolly an improvement from the real deal, ya know what I mean? She's caked up with all that makeup!"

Ben remained impassive as Buddy continued his bad advice. "She'd prolly scare a pit bull. Have a beer. You'll forget all about her in the morning. What you need is to find yourself some ready-made ass. Don't have to be no knockout, just Ms. Right Now. Ya follow?" He finished his jab with a raised eyebrow and a self-flattering smile.

Suddenly, there was movement. Ben flung the pillow over his head and rebutted, "No! You are dead wrong, Buddy. I know I may have been quick to proclaim, 'The One' in the past, but this one's different."

"Quick!? No, Wyatt Earp was quick. You, you're something else. Heck, I think last year alone you were almost engaged at least a half a dozen times! Tell me I'm wrong."

"There was something there! Something very different."

"Okay, different. Different how, exactly? Implants?"

Ben took in a deep breath and then continued, "No, not different like implants. Actually, the total opposite. She was natural, witty, sharp. She was honest and nice. She had the cutest English accent, and..." Ben stopped and looked at Buddy with puzzlement.

"And what?" Buddy said.

"Why are you looking at me like I have a third eye, six noses, and antennas?"

"I'm not, you paranoid crackpot. Keep going. This is starting to get good."

"She had amazing curves, from her hips to her cheeks...a one-of-a-kind, drop-dead-gorgeous goddess."

"Okay, okay! Now, we're getting somewhere. I took my meds today, so I'm good. Keep going. Details!"

"You're a sick bastard, you know that?"

"Keep going before I dry up like a limp eggplant and die, for Christ's sake!"

"Okay, hips. She had incredible hips and thighs. She... All of her was like an Athenian princess! Her face was flawless."

"I got it! She was dressed up as Wonder Woman, right? Boobs. How were the knockers?"

"You know, forget it!" said an exasperated Ben.

"What! I can't ask about her pillows?"

Ben grabbed his phone, found an image of Beyoncé, and then showed it to Buddy. "Imagine her with green flesh and a leathery, body-hugging, very revealing intergalactic costume."

Buddy reached for his reading glasses, scratched and held together by duct tape. They usually hung over his forehead, but he almost always forgot where he'd placed them. He studied the image, making lewd comments and sounds then finally exclaiming, "Okay, that right there is one fine Martian!"

Ben continued, "And she took an interest in me. I even..." He trailed off, realizing he was treading into rough water. He had never allowed anyone, not even Buddy, to read his manuscript.

But Buddy kept at him. "Even what?"

Ashamed, Ben admitted meekly, "I even let her read my notebook."

A quiet filled the space between then, tense and undecided.

Buddy finally cracked, "So that's a good thing, right? I mean, you keep that thing wrapped up tighter than a virgin at a convent rally. Shoot, it must be a big deal."

"Yeah, there's some personal notes and memories and stuff... anyway."

"So, this girl got tingly reading your deepest and darkest thoughts? Am I right?"

Ben's eyes did the talking, scanning the room nervously. "See, that's just the thing, Buddy. I don't really know what happened. She seemed really into me and my notebook. She wasn't scanning or speeding through like it was a pamphlet or a weekly circular. She read each and every word, for pages. I'm telling you, man, she was into it! I don't believe for a minute that she was faking it. I mean, why would she? Why go through the whole song and dance?"

"She dug it? It was groovy?"

Ben shrugged. "Yeah, I guess. Seemed so…"

"Jesus H. Christ, this is like pulling teeth with chopsticks! I still don't see what's the big deal!"

"So, just as she was getting to some real juicy stuff, the meat and bones of the action, this Prince Charming guy comes from nowhere and she changes her tune real quick, too quick. In a freaking snap! I think they were together."

"Say no more. I get it. It all makes sense now. Every hot broad has got to be with some bigheaded dick. It's like a rule or something."

"Okay, we don't say 'broad' anymore!"

"Whatever! You know what I mean."

"The way they looked at each other, the way they talked… For sure, there was something strange going on."

"Look, fuhgeddaboudit! There's plenty of fish out there. You got a lot going for ya. Sounds like trouble, anyway."

Ben threw up his hands and sighed in resentful agreement. "It's just…there was a…she felt right."

Buddy nodded and said, "Common! That's just your pecker talking." He laughed until he aggravated his cough. After it quelled, he continued, "So, got a lot of junk over there?"

Ben sat unresponsive, still locked in his thoughts.

"Hey, kid. I'm gonna' make some soup. Ya' want some?"

Ben shook him off, then broke out with, "You know when there's someone out there who changes the lighting in the room. It's like they opened a small window into a whole universe of happiness."

"Yeah. I opened that window three times. Heck, everyone's gotta' get divorced at least once, am I right?"

Ben clearly was in no mood for Buddy's crass humor. But he knew his roommate was trying. "So, she didn't say anything else to you about the book?"

Ben shook his head.

"You get a number?"

Again, Ben just shook his head. Then, slowly, he reached into his messenger bag, pulled out his notebook, and flipped through the pages. "She got to about here and then—"

Ben paused with a frightful expression. His jaw was locked in astonishment as he held up a business card.

Buddy pressed, "What's that?"

Ben examined the card and then handed it to Buddy. "I guess she did say something after all."

Chapter Five

Monday morning came and Ida was at her desk in her corner office, busy typing and reviewing stacks of reports. She paused to stare at her stack of business cards in the holder on her desk. In this electronic age, hardly anyone had business cards anymore. But Ida felt it was always good to have a couple on hand, just in case. In-person meetings were a dying form of contact. These days, web meetings were all the business world needed. A dependable, fast-connecting phone was the critical device for a successful business. She considered it more than lucky that she'd had one business card in her money clip, tucked away somewhere in that tight, posh Gamora outfit from Comic Con.

But it had been three days, and still nothing.

Her office was basic

and uncluttered. There was one mostly barren bookshelf, which held only a few catalogs and binders, and there was a thin layer of dust on those. A sole bamboo plant grew in a fine Ming vase by the window. There was one other chair opposite her desk, reserved for clients. On the floor was commercial-grade blue carpeting. Beyond that, the office was functional and lacking in personality. The walls were bland, white, and dull. The office's best feature was the extra-large window overlooking the city skyline, a portion of famed Central Park, and the Hudson River. Ida was all business, and the expansive room reflected that.

Consumed by her career, Ida's love life, like everyone else's, was complicated. Her last relationship had well exceeded a decade, and the end date was not quite defined. She'd returned the engagement ring, and though she still had connections, Spencer, by and large, was a non-active person in her life. They had not spoken for over three years now. But the way things ended had left the door cracked open.

Ida was in her early thirties and just now finding out who she was apart from him. Since the breakup she'd felt emotionally immature and lost. At her age, she was well past the cheesy pickup lines and uninspired one-liners; they were an instant turnoff regardless. She had arranged a few blind dates, which all ended with casual "good evenings" and no hopes for a second date. She had been involved with Spencer for over a decade, and still she was uncomfortable moving on. There were loose ends that needed tying and more of herself that needed finding.

She'd found her chance meeting with Ben quite refreshing, stimulating on multiple levels. All weekend she couldn't stop thinking about what she had read in his notebook. There were dozens of touching side notes and memos, which included phrases like, "Include Mom's healing touch and wisdom to use hugs rather than words," and, "Add breathtaking moments of shared silence, where there is only one heartbeat between the two lovers." She was moved. There was permanence. He seemed more in touch with himself than she had ever been. Now, after three days of no contact, she was worried that Kurt's actions, despite being harmless and instructed, may have spurred the aspiring writer away from her.

She pulled her long, silky hair back, tied it, and returned to her computer screen. She tried to break her funk by reading, scrolling, and tabbing like an industrious worker bee. But after only a few minutes, she again found herself daydreaming about Ben. Now the fantasies took on a more primal, sultry twist. His lean body had made that bare-chested costume work, but it held no equal to his chiseled, manly face and endearing eyes. *What was so bewitching about his eyes?* she thought. They were mesmerizing. He was strikingly virile. He was definitely hot. And his personality elevated him from eye-catching to runway model.

It finally hit her: This boy had passion, the kind of passion that was driven but not obsessive. His notebook was a mosaic of clues etched everywhere, years of random thoughts and touching moments. He just needed to craft a story line that would integrate all these elements and he'd have a blockbuster on his hands. She was impressed, and strangely jealous. He didn't run a ladies' man game or tailor his persona after some stereotype. He was unapologetically himself. She finally chastised herself, scolding out loud, "Ugh, there's got to be something wrong with this boy!"

She quickly convinced herself. "He's probably in a relationship, and, true to his nature, he wouldn't want to pursue another."

Now laughing out loud, she declared, "Good heavens, Ida! Get a grip!"

She grabbed the business card display, dropped it into the trash bin, and exhaled.

Minutes later, the voice of Carmen, her secretary, blared through the intercom. "Ms. Shah, there's a Mr. Williams here to see you. He states that he is a showrunner for HBO's *Westworld*, Native American affairs."

Her world stopped spinning in an instant. She stared down at the scattered business cards in her trash bin and whispered an almost inaudible, "Ben?"

Carmen let a few seconds elapse before buzzing again. "Ms. Shah?"

Ida gulped down her hesitation and looked around. Her office was not a setting she wanted to showcase to Ben. It had the personality of a stapler: functional, and not much else. She finally replied, "Carmen, I'll be out in two minutes."

"Very well, ma'am."

She hadn't felt nervousness like this since high school as she fumbled for her pocketbook and clumsily knocked over a stack of folders. She took a quick look at herself in her diminutive makeup kit mirror. Horrified, she whipped out a brush, untied her hair, and stroked like a champion beautician at her bird's nest of a hairdo. She added a few quick touch-ups to her already unblemished face, then inhaled and exhaled several times, each breath slower and longer than the last, until she was calm. She repeated to herself, "Be open, be yourself. Be open, be yourself. Be open, be yourself." That was before squealing, "Holy shit! He's really here!"

She placed her hand on the doorknob and took in three quick breaths followed by one long exhale. Then she turned the knob and slowly opened the door.

There he was, in flesh and blood. Ben stood smiling from ear to ear. Ida froze, as Ben's real self was beyond anything she could have imagined. She screamed in tortured silence, *Oh, my God, he is right here, and he is gorgeous!*

His natural copper tone skin tone was radiant. His angular chin was more defined without the face paint. Those full lips and that joyous smile were bookended by the cutest dimples. She wanted a taste in the worst way. His curled and wavy dark brown hair, hidden by his wig at Comic Con, was of the trendy artist sort. The tips were highlighted with a dark blond. It was pulled back in a man bun, a term she had never given a second thought to before but realized now was perfectly befitting. Ben's five-o'clock shadow added even more depth and scruffiness, as if he needed any. She'd never been into the rough-and-ready type, and now she was wondering why on earth not! Out of his costume, Ben was exceedingly more attractive than she had imagined him to be.

His heather blue lightweight hoodie draped on his square, broad shoulders. The unzipped center outlined a well-defined chest and a lean midsection—no gut bulge at all. A trendy, oversized black leather belt held up his tight fitted stone-gray skinny jeans. He was lean, and the right bulges hinted at powerful legs—and other traits desirable in a man. His high-top black sneakers completed the hip look of this urban hunk. He was an Adonis.

Ida feared she was too smitten, too awestruck, like a child on Christmas morning. She fought hard to temper her emotions, but her elated smile could not be masked. She waved timidly and slowly approached Ben.

All the while, Carmen pretended to be busy with paperwork. Indeed, she was astonished at what she was witnessing. She knew her new boss to be all about business and manners, politeness, consideration. Any form of socializing was unequivocally out of character. She was an administrator, and by all accounts a fine one. She did not engage in office chitchat or familiarity. Usually even the suits had a best friend or confidant, but not this one. She was a loner who always had a smug look and a closed door.

But Ida was not the only one frozen in veneration. Ben was borderline intimidated. In her six-inch heels, Ida stood almost as tall as he. Ben was awed by her natural beauty, admiring her body-hugging business attire. Her navy-blue skirt accentuated the exquisite curves of her legs and those hips that Ben could never forget. The skirt was knee high, revealing toned and sleek legs that shined with her impeccable brown skin. Her calves had a muscular shape to them, firm and athletic.

She strutted toward the waiting area. Every heel strike on the linoleum floor caused Ben's heart to palpitate in anxiety, like approaching the peak of a rollercoaster right before the unwatchable free fall drop. He could not help but notice the curves of her white silk blouse, which cracked a glimpse of her bosom. Its form was more than enough to weaken Ben's knees. Her hips switched from side to side provocatively, nearly causing Ben to pass out cold from dizziness. But it was her gorgeous, stunning face—a sleek, cute nose, scrumptious round cheeks, deep brown eyes, and a pair of full, enticing lips—that finished him off. Her long, straight jet-black hair had a glossy finish and flowed flawlessly. Ben was hopelessly reduced to putty in her hands, as was evident by his puppy dog eyes.

Those eyes melted Ida. Standing toe to toe, each was as awkwardly motionless as the other.

Unlike Ida, who had a more developed ability to mask her emotions, Ben wore his openly and proudly on his sleeve. How could he not!

She parted her lips to speak, with Ben fixated on every minute movement. "Hello then, Benito," articulated Ida crisply and sensually, with a regal, abridged nod.

Ben retuned with a more cracked and underwhelming high-pitched, "Hey."

Carmen had dropped her jaw, and her fingers were frozen on the keyboard. She had traced Ida from her desk to the waiting area, completely engaged, anticipating some sweeping romantic kiss and embrace like from *Gone with the Wind*. Instead, Ms. Idalis Charmaine Shah stood composed.

Ben played it off. "Hello again, and good morning. I just happened to come by and…"

Ida sensed the entire floor gawking at them, so she took the opportunity to interject and make a break for it. "Would you like to go over those figures in more depth and discuss how we can reach a mutually beneficial price point?"

"Ah, sure?" agreed Ben.

"Splendid."

Ida held out her palm and directed Ben toward the elevator. As soon as the doors closed, Carmen grabbed her cell phone and started texting.

Chapter Six

The elevator ride was eerily quiet—descending from the sixteenth floor in complete silence with the soul mate of your dreams was unnerving. It might as well have been a ten-mile drop. Ben and Ida each behaved like schoolkids left frightfully alone with a pubescent crush: staring at anything other than each other, and suddenly losing the ability to articulate. Mostly they kept laser focus on the countdown to the lobby.

As the doors opened to the ground floor, Ida bashfully motioned him off, but Ben's gentlemanly instinct insisted she disembark first. Ida took the lead and proceeded to the lobby's panel of doors. She paused for a second, detoured toward a desolate corner, and said, "So, Ben. This is certainly a pleasant surprise. I wasn't expecting you at all."

"It feels like you're showing me the door, and I get it. But please, hear me out! I intended to call, like, a dozen times, but I felt I needed to meet you in person. When I saw your work address, and I knew I'd be close by, I figured I'd take my chances. Crazy, huh? I know it is, but I'm not a stalker."

Ida laughed. "I should hope not. You would be a dreadfully terrible stalker. There are more cameras here than at JFK, not to mention at least two dozen witnesses and a security staff, albeit largely inept."

Ben hesitated, then blurted, "Okay, so here it is. I thought we hit it off pretty well, and if not, if you were just being friendly, then you wouldn't have left this, right?" Her business card was wedged between his right forefinger and index finger.

Ida's gaze locked onto the card and she released a sound of jubilation, then demonstratively and slowly stated, "I was sincerely intrigued. I wanted to read more." She took a look at Ben's now salvaged and hopeful face. "I pretty much ignore pickup lines. It's standard practice, really. But you actually talked to me. You actually conversed, and you were purely subject-driven and not about your bank account, or your fancy sports car, or how good you could make me feel. You're different, different good. It was the most fun-filled fifteen to twenty minutes I've had in years."

"Oh," was all a relieved Ben could muster.

"Moreover, your pursuit of your passion is admirable. I'm quite jealous, actually. I had hoped to read more and delve deeper into what you're about, but my bodyguard found me and, well…" Ida trailed off as her eyes followed a crowd of suits who had just entered. Abruptly she redirected, "Follow me."

With that, she dashed for the revolving doors and exited the building. Ben was amazed at how fleet of foot someone in such high heels could be. He tailgated her out of the building.

She trotted halfway down the street, periodically looking over her shoulder. As they rounded a corner, Ida panned the streets in a three-hundred-and-sixty-degree rotation. Ben cautiously joked, "You haven't been on *America's Most Wanted*, have you?"

Ida cracked a smile and said, "I must seem like a loon, but, frankly, the office is more of a junior high school than a professional setting."

Ben smiled. "I know the perfect place."

In a welcomed reversal of roles, Ida surrendered to Ben and happily allowed him to take the lead. They quickly ambled down three-and-a-half city blocks, halting at the doorstep of the Abbey May Bookstore. Ida read the name aloud and looked genuinely delighted. "A bookstore? Of course! I had no idea there were any of these left."

Ben opened the door and proudly exclaimed, "I'm always amazed by how many people don't know this place exists. It's one of my favorite hideaways, and one of my gigs. We stay afloat mainly due to specialty online orders, and lots of rare books. I'd be a mess if it ever closed."

As they entered, the cashier, a perky, young, hip woman with a nose ring, eyebrow piercing, and more tattoos than uninked skin, greeted him. "Hey, Ben, you're here early."

"It's all good, Pearl."

Ida took a moment to scan the store. It had personality and charm that mirrored Ben and his writing. *This must be his second home,* she thought, and how befitting. There were three antique armchairs at the end of three long, wooden bookshelves. Each wore the wear of use well, maintaining elegance and stateliness. The craftsmanship of the woodwork trim was striking, and its dark finish gleamed. The floors were marble, mostly white with black swirly lines, and bore a more-than-century-old sepia tone. Ornate chandeliers gave off a bright yellowish glow. The umbrella stand, side tables, wall art, and even the cashier's desk were decorated by antiques or were antiques themselves. Red velvet drapes tapered with gold twisted ropes and tassels harkened images of early twentieth century playhouses. The mood was extraordinarily warm and cozy. One could easily get lost reading a timeless classic or a recent best seller, and Ida was instantly happily lost here with Ben.

"This place is absolutely wondrous! What a simply precious hideaway!"

"Precious, indeed!" exclaimed Ben as he proudly canvased the store.

"You know, I've worked down the street for nearly two and half years and haven't once noticed this bookstore," said an exasperated Ida.

"Well, now you have no excuse," delighted Ben.

Ida smiled, again pleasantly surprised by this captivating fellow.

Ben knew the mornings at Abbey May saw little foot traffic, and even fewer roaming patrons. It was the perfect private time. He motioned to Ida. "Come here."

She followed him past the last row of bookshelves and toward the back of the store to a partitioned, squared-off area. As they approached, she was enveloped by the unmistakable aroma of tea and coffee and exclaimed, "Icing on the cake!"

Ben stopped, nodded, and presented a small table housing a Keurig coffee maker and an electric hot water heater. Adjacent to the brewing machine was a rack of assorted coffees and teas and a silver tray of milk, cream, and sugar. Beside it, under a glass bell, was an assortment of biscuits and biscotti. Even the beverage tray and condiments were antique silver, spurring Ida to comment, "Queen Anne silverware and an enviable array of teas. Did we just fall out of a rabbit hole? However, did you find this place?"

"I think the owner is from London. That, or she wants to be. She's got good taste."

"Clearly," a rather impressed Ida remarked.

Hanging on a nearby wall was a miniature wooden house crafted with intricate detail. A window shutter was cracked open, and a sign hung underneath it that read, THE BEST THINGS IN LIFE ARE FREE, BUT NOT COFFEE AND TEA. DONATIONS WELCOMED. THANK YOU. To which Ida commented, "Oh, now that is clever!" She let out a hushed, adorable laugh, like a child would. Ben was elated that Ida was genuinely impressed. She had abandoned the cold, clinical demeanor she'd displayed in the lobby of her office building, and the twinkle that had hooked him was back.

She chose a chai latte and proceeded to pour in a splash of skim milk. He brewed a decaf coffee and took cream and sugar. They sipped their respective beverages in content silence, smiling and relaxing into the quiet.

Ben purposely avoided inquiring about the Comic Con bodyguard, Kurt, although he desperately wanted to learn more. Moreover, he wanted to know more about Ida. "So, I assume you don't run copies or cold call clients about exciting new offers. Unless you do, then in that case there's nothing wrong with it, except that's a real expensive suit for that kind of work."

Ida was amused—and complimented. "That's very open-minded of you, and refreshingly nonjudgmental." She took in a deep, preparing breath and then continued, "I'm a director of medical sales at OrthoBeta International, specifically new products, beta testers. It's what I do, and it has its rewards as well as its wants." She lowered her eyes, saying much by not saying more.

Ben nodded and added, partially confused, "That's fabulous, isn't it? I mean downright kick-ass for, what? Twenty-two- or twenty-four-years young?"

Ida glared at Ben, causing him to hold up his hands in defense and apologize. "I'm sorry! I mean eighteen!"

She finally deflated his angst with laughter. "I'm flattered by the former, but the latter is just outright insulting! I'll be thirty-three come February of next year."

"No way! And I'm not just laying it on thick. Really, you look at least a decade younger. Like a breathtaking twenty-one-year-old, fresh outta college!"

Ida blushed at the compliment. "And yourself?"

Ben stuttered, then plainly said, "An old soul of twenty-eight, going on twelve."

Ida nodded with a hint of trepidation but continued, "Oh, my. I'm robbing the cradle, aren't I?"

Ben blinked in exuberance and awkward flattery upon realizing her romantic allusions. He smiled and succumbed to his fears. "So, is your bodyguard some psycho ex or something?"

Ida chuckled. "That would be highly improbable. He is very, very, very not into women. But he is my best friend, and possibly my only true confidant. He looks after me quite well. I should do more of that for him, but he really doesn't require looking after, nor would he accept it." Her tone took a more serious turn. "Truthfully, I did ask him to serve as a cockblocker of sorts. I've just ended a long-term relationship, and I thought it fitting to enlist Kurt to stand guard and allow me to be me for a change. I wanted to actually enjoy myself without swatting flies, whom I seem to be attracting lately."

"Wait, hold up—"

"Apologies. Present company excluded, of course." Ida suddenly broke eye contact and took a moment to gather her thoughts, a tall order for someone so well-worded. She finally looked up, stared off at the nearby bookcase, and spoke plainly. "I discovered many things about myself. First and foremost, I need to know what I want for myself before I can be there for someone else."

Ben felt the cold rush of his old nemesis resurface: a crippling, overactive nervousness accompanied by a petrifying, suffocating anxiousness. It had a way of overtaking Ben in times of emotional distress.

Ida continued staring at the bookcase and added, "So, I spent some time traveling, dabbling in some fine arts, cooking classes— what a disaster that was—astrology…. I even purchased an expensive telescope that I've used exactly one time. But I realized at some point that all those things were sources of happiness from without, not from within."

Ben's anxiety subsided amid Ida's personal revelations and he offered, "I get it. Been there. I've heard it said that there are only two days in the year that nothing can be done. One is yesterday, and the other is tomorrow. Today is the only day to believe, love, and live."

Ida reestablished eye contact, and they shared a stunned astonishment as they stated in unison: "Said the Dalai Lama."

"You've read his book?"

"Only all of them," replied Ben, as he pointed to a section of the bookshelf labeled "Self-help."

At this, Ida smiled. "You are a fascinating, charming young man, Mr. Benito Williams."

"Please, we're a few years apart, nothing more. I'm just a guy who is still charting his way through murky waters himself."

"From what I read, you show promise and maturity beyond your years. You're surer of your direction than I am of mine."

"You know what my roommate once told me?"

"What?"

Ben used his best old-man voice to imitate Buddy: "If you wanna make God laugh, tell him your plans for the next ten years."

Ida was absolutely intrigued—and undeniably aroused—by Ben.

They spent the next few hours chatting about the philosophies of Aristotle and Locke and Buddha. They shared stories from their respective childhoods and teen years. They compared their top five dishes, top five drinks, and their top five least favorites of each. In a short time, they bonded. They found similarities in each other's core personalities and, above all, found they shared a thirst for more out of life.

Ida couldn't hide her growing admiration for Ben's pursuit to be a writer despite financial setbacks and a traditionally grounded career path. The more he spoke, the more she sank into a romanticized view of the world and how things should be. He was a dreamer, and an unapologetic one. He was also a thoughtful and astute listener, not only asking pertinent questions, but relating them to historical and current events while citing books of every genre left and right. To Ida, who considered herself well-read, Ben was slightly intimidating. But he never came across as a know-it-all, nor arrogant. Endearingly, he conversed with a sincere and tender heart.

Her sharp, quick wit was easy to captivate. Her genuine charm and charisma screamed leadership and exuded reassurance that someone exemplary was steering this ship. He found that extremely enticing. Among many of the attributes that furthered his attraction was her absolute attention to him. Why in a million years would this overachieving rising star of the business world hang onto every word he had to say, laugh at his every joke, and spend nearly three hours of her surely hectic and demanding day in a quiet little bookstore with underachieving Ben? His insecurities threatened to creep in, but here, in her presence, his ghosts lost their haunt.

Suddenly, the antique German cuckoo clock on the front wall chimed, and two woodsmen slid out of open doors, chopped the air with their axes, and then quickly retreated.

"Oh, my," startled Ida.

"It's noon; my shift begins."

Ida gasped in fright and looked at her Movado wristwatch. "Goodness, how time has flown!" She held her palm to her mouth in apologetic and slightly bubbly laughter, the kind princesses are often taught.

Ben remained speechless, still smiling but saddened by the end of the magical morning.

Ida fought the urge to stare at only the floor, a defensive mode she often employed, but something moved her to be direct. She would not close this door. She declared, "I enjoyed this immensely, and would like to do it again, if you are free as well…."

Ben stared into Ida's intense eyes and uttered, "Um…"

She retracted in embarrassment, scanning the floor. "Oh, my! How presumptuous of me. I just assumed…"

Ben clasped both of his hands over hers, immediately sending sensual jolts throughout her body. He cleared the air with a stern declaration: "I'm here again Thursday at the same time. See you then."

Ida smiled and nodded, trying to mask the euphoric explosion within.

Chapter Seven

Once Ida made her swift exit from the Abbey May Bookstore, Ben dragged along the floor she'd walked on, staring as though he was starstruck. He pitted himself against the glass doors and watched as she faded from sight. That had been the most exhilarating first date of his life. He couldn't even remember his first date ever, or who he lost his virginity to. None of that mattered on Cloud Nine.

Pearl threw shade on his sunny day, mocking from a distance, "Hey, Romeo, you gonna clean up that drool? I spent a good five minutes sparkling up that glass. Some dignity, please."

Ben ignored her usual brashness and remained pinned to the window.

Pearl placed her book down and barked, "So what was that all about, anyway? She suing you or something? Cause she looks like a lawyer or something with fangs and claws. I mean, that power suit costs more than my rent, and my room ain't cheap! Even though I share it with four other assholes."

Ben apathetically waved his hand.

Finally, Pearl circled around her desk and approached Ben. She examined him briefly before unleashing a mild whack upside his head.

"Hey, what gives!" jolted Ben.

"Snap out of it already! Gross."

"You're nuts, Pearl."

"I've seen starving dogs behave with more dignity."

"What's your problem?"

"Dude, I'm being nice, okay? But if you wanna play the slumming pool boy role, be my guest." Pearl folded her arms disapprovingly, shaking her head. "She's way outta your league, *muchacho!*"

After a long pause, Ben surprised her with agreement. "I know, which is why this is so mind-blowing! Dude, she hung out with me for nearly three hours! Three whole freaking hours! With me!"

"That's what I'm saying. Pity usually lasts for about three minutes. Shoot the shit, then ease him down gently and slip away. Three hours, I dunno; that shit's just crazy."

Ben proudly jabbed, "And we're doing it again on Thursday!"

"What!"

"Yeah, I know."

"How did you guys meet?"

"At Comic Con! We chatted for a while. We really hit it off."

"I'll say you did. Did you strip for her or something? Show off those rock-hard pecs of yours?"

"No!" Ben was defensive until he thought about it. "I was bare-chested but covered in body paint."

"Uh-huh," grunted Pearl. "Who knew Comic Con was such a meat market?"

"Please, it's not. I've never met anyone at Comic Con, and I've been going for ten years!"

"I've never gone. I guess I should go to the next one.... Wait, didn't you go as that terrifying Native American with the bloody handprints?"

"Most def!" Ben proudly proclaimed. "Why?"

"I knew it. You posted a selfie on Facebook or something. I thought it was badass!" said Pearl before she probed, "And was Ms. Fancy Pants dress up as Maleficent or something?"

Ben sensed this conversation heading down a twisted, uncomfortable, dark road. Pearl was teasing him, but really she was flirting with him, taking the defensive adolescent approach. She always did that. But Ben was never really interested. He knew he had to proceed with caution. "She went as Gamora, a totally legit costume! She was really into *Saga* and, you know, we got to talkin and—"

"And she handed you her business card and wanted to meet up, right?"

Ben was bewildered. "Yeah? How did—"

"Oh please. That's the move. I'm just wondering why she didn't take you to the Four Seasons to seal the deal, is all."

Ben shrugged Pearl off but wanted desperately to shake his swollen head and wave his defiant finger at her petty attempts to spoil his perfect day. He was surer than anything that the last three hours had been far superior to any one-night stand. He was head over heels just being with Ida, intoxicated by everything about her. And soon they would see each other again.

•

Ida was nearly skipping as she exited the elevator on the sixteenth floor and floated into her office. Only the taps of her expensive high heels alerted anyone to her presence. She made no effort to contain her spritely smile. Carmen again tracked her boss from entrance to exit with half-dollar-sized eyes. Ida was greeted at her office door by five Post-its. She plucked each one off while subtly singing some unrecognizable but melodic tune. She removed each Post-it in rhythm, ending with a spinning pirouette to punctuate the performance.

Carmen thought for sure that Ida was on some drug trip. The minute Ida closed her door, Carmen took to her phone again, stealthily texting with the fury of a courtroom stenographer.

Inside her office, Ida took off her overcoat and wrapped her arms around it as though it were Ben. She leaned on the door and closed her eyes, imagining he was right there with her. Bits and pieces of their conversation swirled in her head. There are few times in one's life that a conversation leaves such a deep impression, and she knew she would never forget it for the rest of her days. There were so many tidbits of information interspersed with jokes and laughs and quotes and nods. Her cheeks were actually strained—not by forced smiles, like at weddings or graduations, but by unfeigned enjoyment.

She knew that these moments weren't about remembering exact words, or the sound of the German cuckoo clock, or the aromatic teas, or the antique furniture. These moments were unforgettable in terms of the fluttering butterflies, the ember stoked into a roaring flame in the pit of her stomach, a stomach that had been hungry, growling with resentment. Nothing could bring her down. She was walking on air.

And his touch at the end, the way he'd held her hands in his, which were manly, yet tender... The corporal connection had unleashed a tornado of emotions. It was the perfect ending to the most perfect early morning first date ever.

Only one feeling blemished the daydream: she was raging for more. The need tore her apart. Why had he not just grabbed her and kissed her with those inviting, juicy lips, lips that spoke words that had melted her, unlocking years of self-imposed isolation!

Ida scolded herself for acting like such an adolescent, but she forgave herself in the same breath. She had never spent three hours in such enchanted conversation with anyone. And now she could not for the life of her transition back to work. Usually, she could always flip the switch, straighten out, and refocus, no matter the cataclysmic event. What had this boy done to her!? Whatever it was, she was all bent out of shape, and uncharacteristically behind in her workload. She needed caffeine to help shake herself free from the whimsical, dazed procrastination.

She arranged the Post-its on her desk in one neat row and stared at them blankly for a long time. The old Ida was creeping back. She became ultra-focused, and the wheels of management churned into attack mode. She quickly hatched responses as she scribbled notes on each.

The very last Post-it paralyzed her for a few seconds. It simply read: *Eddie called 11:38 am.*

Ida knew about a dozen Eddies, but only one who doesn't leave a last name. It must be Eddie Cartwright, as in Eddie her ex's brother. *Oh, lord, why did he call* she brooded. She always held Eddie in high regard. She had not severed all ties to her past abruptly but distance over the years had practically accomplished the same thing. Still, he would never call unless it was important and he's a kindhearted soul. The wet blanket effect damped her cheerful state as sunk into her chair.

Then, a glossy, laminated card of some sort caught the corner of her eye. It gleamed out of her coat pocket.

Ida curiously pushed back on her chair and stood up. She peered at it, then prudently approached her coat. When she withdrew it, she realized it was part of a poem, *Someday I'll Love by Ocean Vuong*. It ends with a comforting thought of loneliness but still part of this world and beautiful touching philosophical metaphors about life and direction. It was thoughtful and profound.

This warrior proved a most formidable foe she thought *and resistance might prove futile*. She blinked like a flickering campfire and then dialed Kurt immediately.

Chapter Eight

On that Thursday, Ben arrived at the Abbey May Bookstore a half hour early. He had worked out a deal with Pearl, his meddling supervisor, for him to knock out most of his inventory duties in order to clear an extended break time. Initially, he considered blocking off about half an hour, but time ran away like a locomotive past its deadline.

Pearl was shocked to see him enter the bookstore. "Wait, what? I thought you were off today."

"I am," confirmed an assured Ben.

"So, like, you're having your second date with Miss Thang *here?*"

Ben simply nodded, paying little mind to Pearl, who just shook her head and rolled her eyes.

Meeting Ida again was more nerve-racking than before, with a hint of anxious queasiness. But he chalked up the tension to budding romance.

Interestingly enough, Ben's passion to write had been rekindled. Since Monday, Ben had been writing feverishly. He'd even bought a large poster board and drafted a few diagrams of where his story's arc was heading. By the first draft, he knew exactly where he wanted to take his character.

He had also gone back to his carpe diem attitude, which had lain dormant for many years. It had previously been an integral part of who he was, and Ida's infusion had unearthed it. He bought Buddy an electronic neck massager. He popped by his friend Arty's place of work unannounced, and they had a street-meat lunch from an Asian-fusion food truck. He helped a complete stranger gather leaves, as autumn was in full bloom.

The doldrums of working and life in general tended to compound his bouts with depression. His was not as severe a condition as others' but, nonetheless, he sought a therapist for help. He had been seeing her for a few years, on-and-off, and with her help, Ben was able to cope better and manage his depression. He was prescribed medication, namely a benzodiazepine (Xanax) which sat unopened on his dresser. He had seen many lives dictated by addiction, and that fear was exponentially worse than any anxiety or depression he felt.

His therapist, Dr. Lana Hoda, would say things like, "In all phases in life, even the direst, we have options, we have choices. Too often, we pass judgment on ourselves harshly. Clarity is a monumental achievement. Engage in cleansing, meditative breathing. Empty out all the minor distractions in your life. That way, only the heaviest will remain, and then it will be easier to deal with."

She gave him some self-help books, many of which stressed that the most effective treatment was a support staff. But he had few close relatives, and no siblings. He had a wealth of acquaintances, but in the whole world he had only two real friends: Meck and Arty.

But the most powerful therapeutic advice she had given him was: "The ultimate key to a happier you, is you. Finding inner peace means more than any mantra, more than a book, and definitely more than a pill."

Dr. Hoda went on to say that while there are patients who do need such medications, Ben might not. It was all a matter of building up his self-esteem, his positive thinking. He needed to embrace life and try to move on easily from adversity. And she was right. Ben had immediately embarked on a journey of self-inspection and positivity. He read the books, watched the videos, and attended counseling. He had been inching his way to happiness when he met her, but Ida had given him light speed capabilities.

Few things in life were easy. Arguably, the hardest thing in life was love—but now that was seeming easy. Just "follow your heart."

Yesterday, Meck and Arty had stopped by to badger Ben about ditching them at Comic Con, and to just generally give him a hard time. He was supposed to meet them at the Funko Pop toy booth, which was huge and illuminated. You could basically see it from anywhere. But the traumatizing event that was Kurt had derailed his plans. Ben explained to his friends that, rather than play the wet blanket role the rest of the day, he'd thought it better to call it a night and sulk alone in his humble abode.

Meck was an aspiring filmmaker and a writer himself. Towering at six foot seven, people often mistook him for a basketball player. In reality, Meck had two left feet and some of the most awkward hand-eye coordination humankind had ever seen. His height had always been more of a curse than an advantage. He secretly wished he was average height, able to appear in a crowd relatively unnoticed. But that was not his lot in life.

Meck and Ben met years ago, at the City University of New York. Both men were still trying to find their ways, and although each had a well-defined interest, a career was something neither had committed to. But one can't be a student forever. That just won't pay the bills. Meck and Ben had all kinds of young-men pipe dreams about starting their own business: a food truck, a clothing line, and even a YouTube video channel. But these aspirations were more rooted in one-in-a-million success stories. They were more glamour than reality.

One night, at an art exhibition, they met Arty. Arty was an up-and-coming performance artist who used anything available to make his art. He was smooth, a trained dancer and very athletic. He always drew a crowd and eventually garnered a huge following.

That night, after Arty's performance, the three bonded over beer pong. They have remained tight ever since.

They are all pop culture enthusiasts, each constantly boasting expertise in the pulse of the people. And each can hardly agree on anything, except the fact that friendship means brotherhood. No matter the circumstances, they always have been and always will be there for each other.

Through the years, they have grown busy due to life, but never distant as friends.

Arty created one masterpiece a year, and then eventually none at all. He got a part-time job at a prestigious steak house on the Upper West Side. As time wore on and hours increased, Arty dropped school and worked full time, rising from busboy to evening head waiter. The hours are late but the cash was great.

Meck works the early morning shift delivering cold cuts and cheeses. It's great money, but backbreaking work. He's up by 3:00 a.m., out the door by 3:15, and humping meat all over the city before sunup. The union has been good to him, and he can enjoy other things, like playing video games, watching sports, and sleeping. But even for the behemoth of a man he is, he's one bad back strain away from early retirement.

Ironically, although they share an apartment together, due to their respective crazy hours they hardly ever see each other.

After finally slogging through the lengthy details of Ben's New York Comic Con, his two confidants were silenced. They knew about his mental health struggles and understood what a crushing a blow Kurt must have been for his psyche, so they decided to pass on the inquisition they had planned, but not before Meck stressed that the tickets had not been cheap, nor easy to come by, and that hanging out these days required more work than a few spontaneous phone calls.

He also wanted to know more about the newfound love interest.

Arty was supportive, as usual, but advised against diving too deep just yet. "Enjoy the shallows first."

Ben vowed to try.

Back at Abbey May, Ben looked at his phone with growing nervousness: 12:05 p.m. He and Ida had agreed to meet at noon. His heart started to race as he fought the fear that he was being stood up. He remained in the doorway like a starving hawk, eyeing every direction, immediately shifting toward any signs of movement, whether it be foot traffic, a vehicle, or a flock of pigeons. He had been acting as the bookstore's unofficial doorman for the past fifteen minutes. The angst was building and sweat started to bead on his forehead.

In the background, Pearl couldn't help but tease him. "Oh, that's her right there!" Then she'd quickly apologize, mocking, "Oh, so sorry, that was just the Amazon delivery guy."

Ben largely ignored her, as their give-and-take relationship consisted of 99% sarcasm. But after the tenth snide remark, Ben had had enough. He turned around to deliver Pearl an epic tongue lashing when the door gently tapped him on the back. As he turned, there stood Ida, easing all his apprehension with that smile. She hesitated before saying, "Forgive me, I've been running late, which is absolutely uncharacteristic of me. Against my better time estimations, I stopped to pick up some things to munch. Is the bookstore closed?"

Ben—and Pearl—stood frozen at the sight of her.

It was Pearl who finally broke the silence. "No, come on in." She pointed to Ben behind his back, then swiveled her fists under her eyes, communicating that he'd been heartbroken, almost crying, as he'd watched the clock tick past 12:00. It pleased her to see Ida react with slight abhorrence.

Ida forced a smile, but she was visibly embarrassed. She hated being late.

Ben finally snapped out of his gaze and greeted, "No, nothing to apologize for. Come in. Right this way!"

He led her toward the back, to the small café table and two chairs, where he had placed a centerpiece rose in a paper cup. The rose was beset by two mugs, each on a lace doily. One had tea prepared exactly the way Ida liked it, and the other held his coffee.

Ida was charmed by the thoughtful gesture and remarked after taking a sip, "Ahh."

Again her graceful smile buckled his core as he fumbled over his words. "I…I tried to remember how you took your tea. It may be a little cold."

"Nonsense. It's perfect."

The two enjoyed seconds of tranquil quiet, lost in their beverages and in each other's presence.

Then Ida began unpacking a brown bag, laying out two sandwiches. "You had mentioned a particular predilection to bacon, otherwise you'd be a dedicated vegetarian. Admittedly, that would have been cause for me to abandon ship. I love my meat! So, I present to you the finest BLT that the 5th Avenue food truck had to offer."

Ben was floored, not just by her bringing lunch, but remembering a detail such as this, one of thousands expressed during a densely packed three-hour exchange. He replied, "Thank you. You're so thoughtful."

Ida tilted her head and arched her eyebrow at the rose. "No, this is thoughtful." She waved her palm at the romantic setup. "The sole purpose of the sandwiches was so I wouldn't eat alone. This required clever thought and personalized touches."

Ben was wonderstruck again at her words, captivated by her wit, diction, and that sultry British accent. As they ate, they exchanged glances and funny faces like grade-schoolers in a cafeteria. They were quickly growing more comfortable with each other, and more at ease—so much so that they began playing footsie under the table.

After consuming every last crumb, Ben remarked, "I haven't had a sandwich this good since my *abuela* made me one. Actually, she makes the best food ever."

Ida asked, *"Abuela,* that's grandmother, correct?"

"Yeah, she's Puerto Rican. I'm a combination of Afro-Latino, Native American, and Spanish. I mean, my ancestry report basically checked off half the globe."

"Fascinating! I probably checked off the other half."

"Really?"

"I'm Pakistani and English on my mother's side, and Filipino on my father's side."

"Get out!"

"Together, I think we comprise the world."

"We surely couldn't hold all those flags at once."

"Agreed, but it would make for a rather eye-catching quilt, wouldn't you say?"

Ben took a minute to bask, gazing into her irresistible eyes before inhaling the strength to broach a topic that could end this euphoric ride. But he could not stave off the question any longer, as it had begun to weigh heavier and heavier on his mind. Not asking would surely cause implosion. He'd had little sleep in the last two days as his brain examined every possible approach. So, directly and awkwardly, he asked, "Are you spoken for?"

Ida was taken off guard. She held her mouth agape and her head cocked back. But her eyes betrayed her as they pinballed, searching for a response. "Spoken for? Now that's an expression seldom used. "

Ben looked like she had just shot his dog—not that he had one. He would have made a pathetic spy with a short-lived career, as his face could hide nothing. It wore a look of regret as he said, "I'm sorry; that was too forward. I..."

Ida quickly recovered. "No, why not address the elephant and it is quite fair." She drew in a steadying breath. "I am officially single. I'm not bound to any person but myself." She spoke defiantly, almost defensively. Then she took in another breath and regained her softness. "To clarify, and in the spirit of true transparency, I was involved in a long-term relationship for nearly all of my adult life. I... we continued despite a contentious and tumultuous ride, and were even engaged, for all the wrong reasons. We—correction, I have not been involved since. That was nearly three years ago. Actually, I've been dating myself, although that hasn't gone well either."

A sudden sadness overcame her, and though Ben put on his happiest face, he may have been sadder. He was about to offer some comforting words, but Ida continued, "He was committed to something else. If it were his work, his career, I would have been tolerant. But, as it is, he's an addict. Specifically, an alcoholic, amongst other things."

Ben remained a quiet listener, feeling pity but refusing to judge.

Ida resumed, now in a painstakingly slow, tortured pace, "He did attend rehabilitation, and sought counseling after a terrible accident. I know this sounds trite, but it is, honest to God, the plain unadulterated truth: He is ten times more intolerable and a hundred times the jackass clean and sober! There, I said it. I admitted my reprehensible, inescapable self-truth."

Ida looked spent. She was exhausted. She seemed to perpetually exhale, running her delicate fingers through her hair, searching the ceiling for answers while avoiding eye contact.

Ben remained seated and silent, digesting her revelations as she kept on. "I realized many things. Love is not an entity with clear borders and definitions. There is no such thing as a perfect soul mate. Love should be the reason why we do what we do, and all the sacrifices in between. My parents absolutely hated each other, like the north and the south of your civil war. God only knows why they ever decided to marry, much less bring a child into the world. I never knew if I was the cause of their dread or the instrument of their revenge. Either way, I wanted to prove Spencer and I weren't like them, so I stayed as long as I did. Well past due."

Ben was running on a delay, registering her words in one second, digesting them the next, and then needing a minute more to generate a response. Finally, he said, "Love is feeling that you want to help that person and be with that person, pure and simple, and all you can really hope—not expect—to get back is that same love. That's why nothing hurts more. I haven't been the same since my ex-girlfriend left me five years ago. She…I mean, we were pregnant, and she elected to abort. I thought I was okay with it, but looking back, I wasn't. We were young and unprepared, but I would have loved that kid. How could you not? So, I bottled it up, and the resentment came out in all different ways. Regrettable, ugly ways."

Ida welled up, as tears started to trickle from Ben's wide-open eyes.

He continued, "My father used to say: 'The only thing you should expect when you give a gift is that you feel good giving it.' You shouldn't even expect a thank you. In giving, you already thanked yourself."

"He sounds very wise."

"He was the wisest man I knew. But it took me a while to figure out that love is a gift. You should give everything and expect nothing. Anything in return is a bonus. We were young and couldn't see that." Ben had his past in his eye. He stared into nothingness, revisiting some mixed feelings. As he wiped the tears he continued, "We fought all the time. Geez, it got really bad. I guess we would have been terrible parents, anyway. But the kicker is, one day I got home, and she was a ghost. I mean, she packed nothing. She left her shit behind and split. I didn't even get a note."

Ida hesitated. She was at a loss for words, except, "You poor thing. I can't even..."

Ben stared back at her with a look that resonated unresolved pain. "I'm so not the same person I was then. I understand more, and there's so much bullshit out there. I only want the real goods, you know what I mean?"

Ida wanted desperately to embrace Ben. She knew he needed physical release from this emotional anguish. She had born her soul, or as much as she could, and Ben had reciprocated. Neither had thought that heartbreak would be the topic of the day, but it had gone there, and in a big way.

Ben had a sudden realization: "That was when I really stopped writing and started working all the time, to get lost."

Ida looked thoughtful. "That probably was the time to write. Emotions are raw, they need channeling." She proceeded carefully, slowly. "That's what I read in your notebook. The main characters were...you both."

Ben slowly pieced it together. "Well, yeah, I guess. It was mostly an epic tale of a miracle, a baby, and an artificial intelligence war. I mean, the two bodyguards who..." He trailed off.

But Ida finished for him. "Who fell in love after witnessing what this baby meant for intergalactic peace."

Ben was stone-faced, shocked. He had never allowed anyone else to read his manuscript—Ida's eyes were the only other human eyes on the planet to have glimpsed the pages. And, how fortunate for him, she had cracked the code. He couldn't have done it himself.

The silence that ensued was a thoughtful one. Ben was stunned, drowning in the sudden tsunami of self-truth. Ida placed her gentle palms on his cheek and exhaled. "You must have been devastated. But you shouldn't be now. People make their choices. Sounds like you would have been a great father. It was not in the cards, but it doesn't mean you are any less of a person."

Ben let her touch pulsate throughout his body, happily grounding him into the present. He placed his hands over hers and said, "I've found myself, and now I'm glad I found you."

Chapter Nine

After an extended two-hour lunch, Ida headed back to her office in a clouded, dreamy state, walking through an intersection as a taxicab screeched to a halt to avoid hitting her. She carried on with an unwavering smile as the driver cursed and gestured offensively.

She and Ben had kissed like teenagers with their first loves. Thereafter, they were all over each other—if not for the public, they very well may have stripped down to their skin and indulged their savage passions. But several overly pronounced coughs from Pearl had finally slowed their steamy session to an abrupt halt.

Ida had left him with these words: "I'd like to see you again soon, very soon." She had surprised herself with how forthright she was. She was typically direct in everything other than relationships, but in this young romance, she wanted to be absolutely clear. Shooting straight from her heart was liberating.

She knew she was a type A personality, at times a chore to deal with, strongly opinionated, and rigid. But Ben seemed like the perfect complement—attentive, supportive, and constructive. He listened sincerely. He shared his own trials, and his flexibility and patience had allowed her to be herself without fearing consequences. She thought *this must be what adult conversation was supposed to be about.*

But all that was a backdrop to their kiss.

After she glided into her office, she shut her door, collapsed into her chair, and twirled around, giddy. It had been nearly two hours since that kiss and she was still brimming with Cupid's afterglow, his arrow squarely impaled into her thumper.

Carmen, of course, had quickly texted all her officemates about the hearts in her boss's eyes. She was enjoying being the hub of the office rumor mill.

Ida finally allowed her chair to slow to a stop as she gazed out her office window toward the bookstore. She relived their kiss, a culmination of mutual desire since meeting at Comic Con. All her anticipations had been surpassed by leaps and bounds. After he said he was glad to have found her, Ida grabbed hold of Ben and drew him close. They paused, inches from each other, and stared for seconds, communicating one shared thought. Then Ben leaned over the table and drew her in. He ever-so-softly met her lips, tender and wet and with the perfect amount of pressure. Their very first lip-lock had surged a radiating heat down through her midline and everywhere in between.

Their lips tested the waters for only a few seconds before giving way to the hard-pressing forces waiting to be unleashed. The table only got int heir way as each rose up and sidestepped to open space where, their bodies could meet. Within minutes, his talented tongue met hers, which seemed even more talented. Breaths intensified, and the kiss deepened. He slid his hands onto her face, touching for the first time those tempting features of her cheeks, chin, and earlobes. Their hearts beat at top speed, and the silence echoed only their heavy breathing. Soon their faces radiated with feverish heat.

Her eyelids fluttered as Ben stroked her hips and thighs. His hands were big and strong, but not like oven mitts. His fingers were long and dexterous. She grabbed at his triceps, which felt like steel cables, then rubbed her hands up and down his well-defined shoulders. Then she edged her palms over his rock-hard chest. Soon, they engulfed each other. There was just no stopping it. They could have been in the center aisle of St. Patrick's Cathedral at midnight mass and still they would have continued. Attraction at this level superseded God's code of conduct, ten times out of ten.

Ben had groped every limb of Ida's body. His right hand had cuffed her rear end, and he fought with every ounce of his core to go no further. This was a public place, his place of employment, and where he spent most of his free time as well. But place and time were of no consequence when it came to their passion. It was like holding up a ten-ton boulder as someone tickled your armpits. His left hand outlined her side, partially lifting her bra, feeling the weight of its endowment. He could not have held on much longer.

Thankfully—or not—an elderly couple rounded the corner. At first, startled, they retreated, the man more slowly than the woman. But then, from the corner of the aisle, they observed the young lovers. The elderly man slowly slipped his hand into hers as they appreciated a silent, shared, precious thought and a lifetime of memories.

Meanwhile, Ida had buttressed Ben against a shelf. She had one hand hooked onto his belt buckle, stationary for nearly a minute. This was *so* not Ida's modus operandi. She had always conducted herself like a proper lady, with educated dignity. But every second weakened her self-control. She was moments away from tearing off Ben's shirt and unashamedly leaving love marks—or worse. Her inner thigh purposefully brushed up in between Ben's legs, and she felt his unmistakable, rock-hard self. She, too, was at her breaking point.

It was precisely then when Pearl clearly exaggerated her cough. The two unclasped, each looking down for a moment, collecting their thoughts and finding a point of focus. It was like a supersonic jet approaching the sound barrier and then killing the engine. For the extra nudge of Pearl's cough, they were grateful. Things could have gone from great to overreachingly embarrassing. It took quite a while for the two to catch their breath. Heck, a supersonic bullet train can't stop on a dime.

Ben finally reached out for Ida's hand, delicately embraced it, and said, "I can't feel my toes right now, and that's freaking awesome."

Ida was slow to respond but eventually said with a wondrous gaze, "I just had to have a taste."

Ben smiled back. "It was damn delicious."

Ida grinned. "Absolutely scrumptious."

"Do you think anyone saw us?"

"Besides Pearl and everyone else? Honestly, I don't know, and I don't care."

Ben had grinned back with relief and it melted Ida to her core.

Ida ended her flashback with the warmth of the memory still buzzing through her. Someone once told her that the hottest romances ache when you are separated. It's like an addiction you can't shake. If that was so, she never wanted rehab. She wanted more. She even fantasized calling him and demanding he come to her office to continue, to go beyond, then childishly chastised herself. How could she even possibly do that! She would be the absolute spectacle of the office and could possibly lose her job. Still, fantasy lacks repercussion. The only real harm are the inflated expectations.

Chapter Ten

Over the next few dates, Ben and Ida explored New York City's finest pizza places and burger joints in addition to sushi, Indian, Thai, Moroccan, and French hots spots and hidden gems. Ben always offered to pay, yet Ida always insisted on splitting the bill. Sometimes, at fancy restaurants, she'd whip out the corporate card and put it on the company dime. Ben didn't argue much. For him, this was a big step in personal evolution. He'd modified his historically strict, inflexible ways and tried to go with the flow. It worked. He had never been happier, and she was absolutely delighted that her void had not just been filled; rather, every expectation had been blown to bits.

Ben knew words and phrases in nearly every language, and he had an understated, deep comprehension of historical and present-day sociopolitical issues. He led her in salsa, merengue, and even line dancing.

If that weren't enough, on Halloween, at some random dive bar, it happened to be karaoke night. Ben and Ida were dressed up as Jack and Sally, the two main characters from Tim Burton's classic animated film, *The Nightmare Before Christmas*. Secretly, Ben scribbled his name on the waitlist and surprised Ida in an above-average rendition of Queen's hit song "A Kind of Magic." She was already head over heels for Ben, but now she was absolutely terrified that she was defenseless in his arms. She even questioned, for the first time, if she was at all as interesting to him as he was to her. To think she might not be was petrifying.

But every doubt was eliminated when Ben returned to his seat next to Ida and confessed that he had never done that before. In his previous life, such acts had always been met with criticism and deemed childish. His ex-girlfriend had always warned Ben to stay within himself, to set limits and not embarrass himself—and more importantly don't embarrass her by association. He explained that with Ida, he felt empowered to go for it and disregard what others thought, because she always carried herself unapologetically. He stressed that it was she who empowered him to reengage with his writing and get back to the business of living. She had never received such a resounding compliment.

And with that, she signed up to sing as well. Ida knew she could carry a tune in the shower, but it was an entirely different endeavor to sing in front of a packed house of strangers. Although, having all the audience half inebriated and in costume made it easier. Ben insisted that he hadn't meant to pressure Ida into singing, to which she replied, "Nonsense. I do this because I feel no pressure whatsoever, silly!"

She promptly ordered two more shots of tequila and pounded them down as quickly as they came. When the DJ called 'Sally,' Ida wiped her sweaty palms, took hold of the wireless microphone, cleared her throat, and began, "This is dedicated to the one I love."

As Ida belted out those first few words of the song with the same title ("Dedicated to the One I Love" by The Shirelles), Ben kept his composure despite a resonating numbness throughout his whole body. His heart had been floored by the song choice, and his mouth was frozen agape. Synapses were firing in countless directions. But it wasn't the song itself that had entranced him. In fact, he didn't register much of the song. It was the first time that she had uttered the words "I love you"—although in a karaoke song. On stage, the very animated and slightly tipsy Ida pointed to Ben, winked, and blew a few kisses. She was more than a singer; Ida could easily play to a crowd and command a room. As the song ended, applause and cheers filled the packed bar.

The DJ ended with, "Jack, you are one lucky dude! Let's hear it for Sally! Great costumes guys."

The crowd sent her off in raucous applause, and the ever-graceful Ida bowed and blew more kisses to her fans.

When she returned, she tried to slow her breath, fanning herself to cool down. She exalted, "Oh, my God! Did I just do that!? I haven't done that since my college days!"

Ben sat frozen, visibly stunned, as she grabbed a glass of water and chugged it down in grateful relief. Slamming down the empty glass, she remarked, "I hope that was mine. And I'm thankful it was water!" When her breathing finally eased she glanced at Ben, noticing his unnerved look. "Ben, are you all right? Is anything the matter?"

Ben followed with a flurry of head shakes and nods, searching for his words until he eventually complimented awkwardly, "Great song!"

Ida nodded and motioned for the bartender to refill her tequila, then slowly turned to Ben and said, "I know I may not be a forecaster of perfect outcomes. I can be a bit drab and rigid, an unfeeling taskmaster, or a downright nasty bitch if you ask my lazy underlings, but I live in a world of mostly misogynistic males who cling to their power and would love nothing more than to keep me at bay, in my place. I've spent the better part of my adult life in a largely one-sided relationship that checked all the boxes except the one in my heart. You, my dear, fucking rock! I've never felt more alive or happier than I do when I'm with you! You are real, aren't you? That song right there, I meant every goddamn word. I fucking love you, Benito Williams!"

In the chaotic noise of a karaoke bar on Halloween, silence filled the space between them. That emotional unleashing was like the warning alerts at Chernobyl. Ida's drink had arrived, but Ben took her hand gently and placed the glass down.

Shocked, and expecting Ben would say something else entirely, Ida let him draw her close and say, "Let's get outta here."

Chapter Eleven

They waited on a street corner for their cab to arrive. Once inside the vehicle, they never stopped kissing. They kneaded each other the entire ride to Ida's apartment building on the Upper West Side.

It was a huge, granite skyscraper. The doorman greeted them and escorted them through oversized glass doors. Strangely, as they ascended in the elevators to the eleventh floor, they stood apart, except for their hands. It was the first time since the bar that they'd had a sobering moment to catch their breaths and realize that the next step in their torrid relationship was about to unfold—and it was a pivotal one. Ben and Ida were suddenly feeling nervous.

Everything to this point had been blissfully surreal, filled with heavy petting and passionate kissing. But they each had an inner voice that wondered when and if the bottom would fall out on this joyride. The ultimate fear approached as each and every floor illuminated in a cascading, accelerated pace. But relationships like theirs could only sustain the buildup for so long. It really was time to see if the glitz and glamour of the show car matched—or surpassed—expectations. Rubber was about to meet the road.

When they reached the eleventh floor, the doors opened, and Ida gently tightened her handhold and twinkled a smile. She led him out, and they paced down the gold carpeted hallway to apartment 11G. There, she unlocked the door and turned on the lights, while Ben stood in the doorway, awed and tentative.

Ida joked, "The view is better from inside."

Ben slowly entered the luxurious apartment. "Wow, this is amazing!"

Ida cringed. "Please, it's corporate housing. More than half of the furnishings are standard in every unit here. Make yourself at home. I have to desperately tinkle." As she hurried off her voice faded. "There's water in the fridge."

Ben remained where he was. He was a little intimidated by the luxury accommodations, but more so invaded by out-of-control trepidation. He heard Ida flush and the sink turn on. Suddenly, a rush of fears permeated Ben's mind.

Endless questions bombarded his psyche. Did his breath smell? Did *he* smell? Was he too inebriated to perform? How long had it been since he was intimate with someone? Would the rust show?

Ida was by far the most physically attractive woman he had ever dated, and he had never been captivated like this before. He had to pinch himself to make sure this was real, that she was real, he was real and that this was happening. He had fallen so deep into her that he was a bundle of nerves growing more and more frazzled.

Ida yelled out from behind the bathroom door, "Could you grab me a water from the fridge as well?"

Ben moved mechanically, like a robot. He opened the door to reveal a largely empty refrigerator with bottles of water, a few bottles of beer, and a takeout box from the Thai restaurant they'd eaten at earlier that week. He cracked open the box and realized it was empty.

Then he noticed another takeout box, from a Greek place they ate at a week before. It too was empty. And there was a half-eaten Stromboli roll they'd had for lunch a few days ago. Her apartment was immaculately clean, no clutter anywhere. She wasn't saving boxes—she was saving mementos of their dates. Ben himself had done the exact same thing, much to Buddy's dismay. There was a sense of calming comfort in realizing that.

Ben smiled and grabbed two water bottles. Upon closing the fridge door, there stood Ida standing by the bedroom door. Her Sally makeup had been washed away. Hey beautiful hair, which had been hidden by an auburn tattered wig, was up in a bun, fully showcasing her gorgeous face. Her blueish gray stockings and tattered black boots had been kicked to the side. All she wore was the patchwork costume dress, halfway unzipped in the back and barely hanging onto her body, begging to be peeled off.

She bit her lip invitingly and asked, "May I have my water now? I'm quite parched."

Ben tried to breathe while steadily making his way to Ida. He held out a bottle for her. She took it, unscrewed the lid slowly and drank it in one whole guzzle, never breaking her hypnotizing eye contact. Once finished, she licked her lips ever so seductively and dropped the bottle on the floor. Ben's nervousness turned to engorging, primal lust. He looked past Ida into her dimly lit bedroom and tossed the other water bottle onto her bed.

Ben's hands gently found their way to her back, where they finished unzipping her. Her costume fell to the floor, revealing an absolute beauty. Her eyes remained deadlocked onto Ben's facial expression as his eyes bulged and his jaw dropped. She had left her bra in the bathroom and was standing there naked except for a red thong. The curves of her hips and thighs formed a perfect, tantalizing bell. Her breasts were full, firm, with erect nipples. He gulped several times to draw strength as he proceeded to move his fingers onto those nipples and cup her breasts. He wanted her with unbridled potency, now more than ever.

She helped him out of his tuxedo costume, as it fell to the floor, revealing his well-toned, muscular chest, his six-pack abs, and well-proportioned, powerful shoulders and arms. She nearly bit into him. Her hands followed his abdominal trail down to his zipper. There, she unsheathed his belt like a knight returning home from a lengthy battle and flung it across the room with a devilish grin.

They converged in the doorway, kissing intensely, sloppily and ferociously, stopping only when Ida unbuttoned Ben's pants as they crumpled to the floor.

By now the alcohol had worn off, and raw passion took over. Waves of radiating body heat surged between them. Every touch, every kiss, every sense was intensified. Heartbeats thumped out of their chests. The temperature-controlled apartment felt like a lava pit.

She traced her fingers down his sides and onto his rock-hard midsection, finally clasping at his boxer briefs. She detached herself, but only for a moment, as she squatted down and yanked his boxers to the floor. Her right hand felt him there, unmistakable, pulsating and fully engorged. All around he was an impressive physical specimen escalating her intrigue. She stood up and took hold of him, then tugged him to and fro, spinning his head back. She fastened her lips. As Ben arched his back, she descended to his chest and nipple.

Even totally at her mercy, Ben stood her up and slipped his hand down to her thong. Easily he circled around and found her, engorged just the same and lathered. They continued to stroke each other, sending merciless pulses down their legs and in every other direction. The sensation was more intoxicating than any drug.

They paused before climax, though holding back the euphoria was increasingly unbearable. Sweat beaded down his head, and she felt her scalp moisten. She looked up into Ben's dazed eyes, laboring to breathe, her body one fast-paced throb. Ben's chest heaved, accentuating his athletic frame. In the moonlight, he resembled a world-class bodybuilder. He pulled back and took a long look at Ida. Everything was said in silence as Ben picked her up and carried her across the threshold.

Chapter Twelve

The sunlight filtered into the bedroom. Ben lay naked on his back as the morning gently woke him from the deepest slumber he'd ever had. Ida was partially overlapping him, her left side draped over his body. She was in a deep, blissful coma herself, lying face down. Her left arm was stretched across his chest, her head buried into his shoulder. She echoed the cutest little snore.

Only a fraction of her red satin blanket covered him. But that was enough, because, like the temperature-controlled room, everything was just perfect. Ida was almost entirely covered by the blanket, which outlined the curves of a goddess. As he admired her , he relived taking her into his arms and gently laying her on the bed.

Ben had parted her luscious thighs and kissed her right leg from ankle to calf to knee, tickling her a bit. He then moved up, placing more long, succulent kisses the further up his lips traveled. The pleasure was buckling under the pain of the anticipation. The burning desire to take her had been too much to bear.

Ida had quickly clutched his shoulders and brought him up to eye level. Ben playfully resisted and returned to his intended target. She could not deny the magic of his talents as wave after wave of heart-pounding pleasure caused her to use all her might to hoist him up by his hair and heave him over her. This time, Ben acquiesced and slowly entered her. They were engaged in a rhythmic and euphoric union, climbing rapidly. When Ida thought she was about to reach that mountaintop, she edged him over onto his back and rode him to ecstasy, bearing down on him as they both arrived at explosive release. Nirvana!

She'd collapsed onto him in blissful exhilaration, completely spent, clutching his rock-hard body. Ben lay exhausted, completely knackered by the exquisite takeover. He'd tried to relax his curled toes, to no avail. His right hand clutched her voluptuous, juicy butt, and his left hand clawed into the bed sheet. He may have bitten his lower lip. Long after Ida had fallen asleep, he lay there, resonating in tranquility.

In the morning, lost in the outline of her curves, Ben was still dreaming about the evening. There wasn't even an inkling to check the time—that was the last thing on his mind. He wanted this moment to last forever. His mind wandered from last night to the last month, getting to know Ida, sharing his deepest fears and precious memories. He remembered her witty remarks and jokes, and especially her cute British accent. Every word she uttered just sounded different, sexy. Every slight moment with her had touched him in a way that no other moment had. The world had opened up in exponential ways, and this new perspective had changed everything.

He wondered what a life with her would be like. Not just sharing bills, or an apartment, or a lavish wedding. No, he envisioned long walks, vacations around the world, raising a family, meeting her parents, everything and anything. The usually free-spirited Ben started to think about life as a couple, a real, mature couple, who would meet challenges as a team, a unit, as one. He had been down that road before, and he knew about the pitfalls. But there was a stark difference between that past and this present. When he held Ida's hand, it was all different. It was right.

Then Ida greeted him in a cracked warming voice, "Good morning."

Ben whispered back, "Good morning, gorgeous."

Ida rolled her head toward Ben, cracked open an eyelid, smiled, and closed her eyes again. She slowly repositioned herself, sliding her leg right into his crotch. His hip was now wedged between her warm, strong, and seductive thighs. Immediately she felt him salute in grand fashion. She flirtatiously remarked, "Well, and good morning to you too, big boy."

Ben smirked and teased, "Oh, it's all your fault, you know. I'm powerless next to you."

Ida smiled with her eyes still closed, and then gradually caressed his chest. She seemed tentative, but predominantly assertive. "You know, I am *so* not the type to jump into murky waters, but I can't help myself either. Besides, you're not at all murky. You're as clear as a Caribbean beach. You definitely are a pure soul, and I trust you with mine."

Ben kissed her on the cheek and replied, "I'm helplessly drawn to you, and I know there is no place in the universe for me except right here."

She wrapped her thighs around him even tighter and affirmed, "I'm having the time of my life, and I don't just mean last night. I mean every night. Even the ones we're apart, I feel like you're right next to me. This is a first for me."

Ben let out a great exhale and then proclaimed, "I love you so much. It's been so exhilarating being with you, a never-ending high. I want you all the time. I know it's heavy. I know I'm throwing a lot at you. But I can't hold back. This is how I feel. And this is the realest way I can say it."

Ida blinked uncontrollably but failed to stop a few tears from leaking. His words had touched her, and now she was collapsing into him. Ben enveloped her, cradling her as the tears trickled into contagious streams—Ben started to well up as well.

"I know—" started Ben.

"I am so in love with you. I can't express how much. You are so much better at expressing yourself than I. I'm sorry I can't...," interrupted Ida as his words trailed off into a full, all-out cry. He kept his hold on her, firmly kissing her forehead and allowing her to empty her tank of pent-up emotions.

She had bottled up years of family frustrations, a taxing long-term relationship, and the struggles of climbing the old-boy corporate ladder. Finally, Ben had come along to remind her to enjoy life for enjoyment's sake. She had underestimated the emotional chaos that this rare love had caused in her. Without question, it was life-changing—for the better.

Ida managed to slow the bawling and clean up with a pillowcase. She said, "I do apologize. I know I live a complex existence. I *am* complex, and I don't ever want that to wedge a gap between us. So, moving forward, I want us to pledge to never hold back any issue, and just remain the same open people that we are. This is of vital importance to me!"

Ben composed himself as well, then held her hand and promised, "Above all else, I want to be with you through everything. We do this together, day by day. All we'll ever need is each other. No bullshit, and no pettiness. Just us loving each other for who we are."

They sealed it with a kiss—and another round of bliss.

Chapter Thirteen

Ida slipped away after they finished another thorough and intense lovemaking session. She trotted into the bathroom and started to run the shower. Ben's body lay under the blanket, curled and exhausted. His mind was at ease and his soul boundlessly enriched. Physically drained, and with the soothing sounds of bathroom raindrops, Ben happily drifted off into a peaceful nap. He dreamed about being with Ida in a field of golden daffodils as a gentle breeze rippled their white linen clothes. They stood holding hands, laughing, embracing, the happiest people on earth. It was poetic, detailed with vivid images and vibrant colors. In the distance were the sounds of children playing with an equally spirited puppy. The sun warmed their faces and bodies. This was heaven, he fancied.

Then, unbeknownst to him, the apartment doorknob started to turn. Kurt emerged and announced himself obnoxiously, tirelessly complaining about his boyfriend Cartwright and some apparent drama that had unfolded last night or early this morning. He was oblivious to the trail of costume garments littering the carpet, though he himself was still dressed as the Joker, in full makeup. His hair was tinted Kelly green, and his smile was just as menacing as the crazed villain's.

He slid himself onto the bed, right next to the blanketed and sleeping Ben. Ida had drawn the curtains to allow her dear to sleep well. Kurt continued to whine, spewing one trivial gripe after another, like a chain-smoker of complaints.

Offended by the lack of response, Kurt poked Ben's unsuspecting body. When still there was no response, Kurt grew agitated and reprimanded, "You know, it's bad enough I don't get attention from Cartwright! At the very least, pretend to lend me your ear!"

"Answer me you, heartless bitch!" Kurt blared and then grabbed at the blanket and pulled it off completely, like a magician would a tablecloth, exposing the naked Ben.

The shrill, ear-piercing, horrified scream that followed startled Ben awake. Then Ben matched a high-pitched screech of his own. He rolled over to the side of the bed, tumbled off, and hid himself behind the closet door. Kurt was masking his eyes and face with the red satin blanket. In absolute agony, he timidly asked, "Ben, is it? The Native American killer man from Comic Con?"

Ida bolted out of the bathroom, dripping wet and wearing a fuchsia terry cloth bathrobe. After assessing the situation, she began slapping and punching at Kurt's shoulder. "What in blue blazes are you doing here?" she scolded.

Kurt jovially replied, "Oh, honey, please. I practically live here, okay?"

Ben, whose body was still hidden from view, was shocked and beyond puzzled. "What!"

Ida exclaimed, "He absolutely does not! He crashes here from time to time, and he may water the plants on occasion, but he most certainly does *not* live here! He clearly has a wide interpretation of my hospitality."

"Sweetie, don't even go there!" He turned to Ben. "I mean, we're only sex buddies!"

"Sex buddies?" Ben's face was draining of color.

Again Ida struck Kurt again, then reassured Ben, "No worries. He is soon to be very, very dead!"

After another barrage of jabs from Ida, Kurt clarified, "Oh, please. We wouldn't have sex if my life depended on it. She's my BF-BFF, best fucking bitch friend forever!"

In keeping with his gangster cosplay, Kurt picked up a nearby hand towel and threw it at Ben. "Come on, cover up and let's make up. Nice, nice!"

Ida banished Kurt to the kitchen to make coffee. Then she grabbed a towel and handed it to Ben. "Kurt's a bit of a comedian, and a pretentious drama queen. He means well, really."

"Really?" doubted Ben.

"Come now. Hop in the loo and freshen up. I'll fetch us some breakfast."

Still unsettled, Ben grabbed the towel and dragged himself into the bathroom for a quick, revitalizing shower all the while casting the most menacing stare at Kurt. In the background he could hear Ida and Kurt's continued arguing. Oddly, they were like an old married couple.

The shower didn't do much to change his mood.

Ida inspected the fridge and realized there was not much to eat. She asked Kurt to prepare the coffee, and a tea for herself, then ran down to the corner deli for some much-needed nourishment.

Meanwhile, Ben and Kurt were left to get acquainted.

When Ben finally emerged from the bathroom, he found he had nothing to wear except Ida's fuchsia terry cloth robe. He lost himself in its heady lavender scent, which immediately permeated every thought he had. Suddenly he was flashing back to last night, and this morning. Wrapped in her enticing scent, he imagined her skin on his. It settled him a bit, for now.

Then he moped into the kitchen and there was Kurt, sitting by a small round table, texting. Ben's disdain for Kurt had been superficial before, but it had hit a new low in the last fifteen minutes. He pretended not to acknowledge Kurt's existence as he marched toward the kitchen. Kurt displayed a similar aloofness as he typed away on his cell phone. Ben reached for a coffee mug, and then for the coffeepot—it was empty. In his smoldering contempt, he hadn't even realized there was not a hint of coffee aroma in the air. He set the pot back with a noticeably loud clunk. Kurt remained unphased and silently oblivious, consumed by his screen time. Ben proceeded to march out of the kitchen, still pretending Kurt was invisible. They were behaving like seven-year-olds having dueling tantrums.

Ben had just made it to the kitchen doorway when Kurt startled him. "You must have a King Kong-sized package to rope her in like you do!"

Ben smirked; he couldn't help it. Then he did an about-face and glared at Kurt, who remained glued to his cellular device. He replied, "Well, you've seen it, so I guess we can put that mystery to bed, huh, pal?"

Kurt was still swiping and typing feverishly as he responded, "Well, hot bods rarely last. I should know."

Ben rolled his eyes and was about to exit when Kurt reengaged. "You know, Tarzan, she doesn't impress easily—in fact, hardly ever—but she seems absolutely smitten by you. Almost pathetically so."

Ben's anger flared. "What's your freaking problem, dude? Are you jealous or something? Cause I didn't think you cared like that. Unless you do? Maybe you swing from both sides of the plate, and you're done with one way, so you wanna switch things up a bit?"

Kurt finally tore his concentration away from the phone. He laughed in a sharp, theatrical manner, causing Ben's stone-cold face to crack a smile. "Please. Like, never, bitch! Ida is my sister, and our bond is deep and strong. You don't threaten me, honey."

Kurt waved condescendingly and piled on, "And, sweetie, as fine as you may think you are, know this: If you ever hurt her, you *will* have to worry about me. Heaven knows I don't look the part, but I can get all Dexter on you in a snap!" Kurt ended his rant with a dramatic snap of his fingers but failed miserably to make a sound.

Th dead silence was followed by sincere, hearty laughter on both sides. Neither one could contain themselves.

Ben finally took a seat opposite Kurt. Once his laughter subsided to a mere chuckle he said, "Kurt, for reasons besides avoiding getting whooped by you, I don't intend to ever do her wrong. I love the hell out of that woman, and my heart will always be looking out for her. No one can predict the future, and everyone is running from their past. I think the two of us are at points in our lives where we've been there and done that and know what we want, past all the bullshit. Ya know what I'm sayin?"

Kurt was caught completely off guard. He was floored, rendered speechless by Ben's maturity. He had impressed the heck out of him, which is no small task. Unexpectedly, Kurt felt a grain of jealousy and, what's more, the hint of a threat. He felt he might actually lose Ida's friendship (and attention) to a guy who was shockingly more than just a pretty face and a hot body. Ben seemed like genuinely a good guy, and—even worse—and a great friend.

Ben spoke with sincere intentions. "Look, we got off on the wrong foot. I have played the bodyguard role for friends of mine in the past. I know how to block the assholes; I can smell them a mile away. Keep good people from bad situations, right? I get it. So, we good?" Ben offered his hand in a truce.

Kurt was stunned, and Ben reacted faster than he could, but he eventually shook Ben's hand.

Kurt took a moment to consider how to approach what he considered a necessary topic. He wanted to test the waters of Ben's sincerity and gauge Ida's truthfulness. He raised his eyebrow and cautiously proceeded, "So, I assume she told you all about Spencer?"

"Spencer?" repeated Ben with a surprised pitch. "Well, not in great detail, but enough. I know it was a long-term thing, with lots of ups and downs. I know he continues to struggle with addiction and other emotional stuff."

"Yeah, stuff like that...." Kurt paused, calculating, and then asked, "You okay with all that?"

Ben looked bewildered. "With what, exactly?"

Kurt presumed that Ida may not have been completely forthcoming, so he pivoted. "With her past relationship."

Ben pressed, "Look if there's something I should know, let's be transparent. That's what it's all about, right, guy? I mean, if everything is on the table, we can deal with it. We either accept it and work with it, or fold and move on."

"Okay, you're too fucking understanding to be real! Are you, like, a reformed Buddhist monk or something?"

Ben laughed him off. "Look, man. I'm the type that would rather know what and who I'm up against. I wanna know who will do me in than float through life blindly. When it's in my face, it hurts, but thereafter, I'm good. Trust me, when there're loose ends, I'm a mess."

Kurt suddenly regretted opening this can, but he laid it out there, partly because he agreed with Ben. If this relationship was real, then Ben had to know one cold, inescapable fact. Kurt hesitated, but eventually he said, "So, I assume she told you about Brielle? About him having custody of her?"

At that moment, the keyhole turned. The lock was undone, and Ida burst into the apartment cradling two brown bags of food and a cardboard tray of coffee and tea.

"Hey, boys. Hope you've been civil." She glanced at Ben and said, "Lovely robe. Fuchsia is definitely your color!"

Ben looked stoic and accusatory.

"What's the matter?" a bewildered Ida asked.

Ben said slowly, "So, who's Brielle?"

Ida dropped the brown bags, along with her lower jaw.

Chapter Fourteen

Ida unveiled a long baguette from the grocery bag, stormed towards Kurt and began mercilessly whaling on him while Ben stood by, perplexed.

Kurt relentlessly cried, "Ben, run while you still can! Behold, this is the real Ida!"

Finally, Ida stopped, mostly because the baguette was now in pieces on the kitchen floor. She calmly turned to Ben and said, "All that I said to you about my past relationship was in general terms. I was not compelled to expound in detail, mainly because I found not benefit to re-hash a trip down mistake lane. But if we must go down this route, I shall happily oblige."

Ida turned to Kurt with a menacing sneer, "Some people are like helpless devils, leaving trials and tidbits out of context, recklessly sowing seeds of doubt."

Ben looked more confused than ever. But he wanted to put Ida at ease. "I know what you mean. I wanted to spare you some of the gorier details of my past relationship, but all that we are is in part because of all that we were."

Kurt interjected, "Oh, gory details! Do proceed!"

Ida huffed at Kurt's poor attempts at comedic relief. Most of her wanted nothing more than to agree with Ben and move on, but in scanning her heart, she couldn't. If the roles were reversed, she'd want to know every square inch of any crack in the door that should have been shut.

She struggled to speak. "Ben, you've just about told me everything. And I never felt repulsed or thought any worse about you or your past. Yes, at times, less may be more, but I understand you more for having heard it. You are the most open-book human being I've ever had the utmost pleasure of meeting. The very least I can do is reciprocate, as much as I am able to."

Beet red with embarrassment, Kurt felt compelled to attempt reparations. "I spoke out of turn, a poor attempt at humor. You will undoubtedly determine that Brielle is not a big deal after all. It's true that I'm a bit of an instigating devil. Sorry."

Ida lashed out. "A little!" After taking a moment to gather herself, she elaborated. "Spencer and I are over. There is no going back to him. It was over long before it was officially over. But in terms of our final split, I agreed to one condition, which I sorely regret. But at the time, it was a matter of weighing my options. I wanted to be done with him once and for all."

Everyone was silent in that grave moment. Ida and Ben were deadlocked in an unbreakable stare. Kurt's eyes bounced around like a ping-pong ball, going from Ida to Ben and then to the door.

Ida spoke poignantly. "Brielle is—*was* our dog. Spencer so desperately wanted to keep her. I loved her, but she had much more affection for his drunk, pathetic ass than for me, so it was a difficult but clear-cut decision."

Ben was slow to respond, but eventually he said, "There's no such thing as a clean break. I know this very well. I disengaged relationships with people I considered family."

Ida melted in disbelief at Ben's comforting and nonjudgmental words.

Kurt intervened lightheartedly, "Well, you didn't have that many friends to begin with."

She playfully tossed a throw pillow at Kurt, and again silence filled the room. This time, it edged Kurt out.

"Well, I have to be going now, maybe to build a moat or something. You guys seem…" Kurt stopped short of any other words and excused himself from the apartment.

Ben slowly approached Ida and engulfed her in his arms. He kissed her forehead and placed his chin on top of her crown. They held each other tightly, almost squeezing the other's breath out, for what felt like hours.

Then Ida murmured, "I was not actively looking for anyone, but you found me. All along I thought I needed to be alone, to find myself, but I was just lonely and lost." She stepped back and peered into Ben's eyes. "You helped me find out who I am, who I really want to be."

Ben added, "We found each other. I, too, was wandering though, procrastinating on life. Five years felt like five days. That's what happens when you relive a dreadful day over and over. Sometimes people just need a spark to get that engine going."

He inhaled and said, "Buddy used to work on motorcycles, all kinds choppers, lowriders and custom built them too. He used to tell me that no motor is perfect. You fiddle around with it, adjust this, lube that, and tinker around a bit. Sometimes you gotta' give it a swift kick, and other times you caress it and sweet talk it. But when it purrs, smoothly streaking down the road, it's perfection."

"He sounds intriguingly charming."

"He grows on you," chided Ben.

They coalesced again, enjoying being in each other's arms. Then Ben exhaled. "You know, I had someone vanish off the face of the earth. She didn't give a damn about saying goodbye, or even, 'I hate your guts.' At least I'd have something final. Ya know?"

Ida looked up at Ben with sympathetic eyes and a sobering stillness. Then she said, "On an entirely selfish level, I have benefitted from her callous actions. I never expected there would be someone like you waiting somewhere to meet me. Since our first cup of tea at the bookstore, I have wished every second that I had met you instead of him. I wish he and I never existed."

"But then you wouldn't be you, and I wouldn't be me. I guess that's the cosmos's sick sense of humor!" countered Ben.

"Very sick, indeed."

Ida was certain there was something so uniquely special about Ben that no matter what happened, from this point forward, he would always be the love of her life. Ben appreciated that Ida had lowered the steel-curtain fortress around her heart. The slew of mixed emotions was a giant step toward real intimacy—they trusted the fragility of their respective scars in each other's hands.

Still, Ida wrestled with herself. She, too, wanted everything on the table, but she dared not reveal everything right now. If she did, it might just trigger a heart attack. Brielle was much too much already. For now, Ben had just delivered some of the most touching and endearing words she had ever believed in. She couldn't risk losing this dream relationship. But the look of defiance in Ben's eyes, his resolve against her every issue and hang-up, tormented her to the core.

She cradled a pillow and leaped next to Ben. "There's one last thing, and it's critical. It may damn well be criminal. But, if we are who we say we are, I need to tell you."

Ben had never looked more concerned or more serious. "Yes, tell me."

"Here it goes." Ida inhaled and gathered. "I've done one terrible and regrettable thing. There are times it consumes me and keeps me up all night." She steeled herself with a breath before she continued.

"I reported Spencer to the authorities. I had him locked up and assigned to mandatory rehabilitation. I heard him stumble into our apartment in the early morning, drunk and bruised. He had hurt his wrist. After cleaning up his vomit, something urged me to inspect the automobile. It was a wreck, and I thought I saw blood on the outside. My first inclination was a deer, or some other wildlife. But my gut feared something worse, something human. So, I called." Tears were welling in her eyes. "Like a coward, I never told him. For that, I'm an outright snitch. It still weighs on me. After all these years…"

Ben embraced Ida, letting the silence do all the talking.

She began to sob hysterically before lamenting, "Do you think I'm a terrible person?"

Ben replied, "Never. I think you were in a tight spot. Your support couldn't be a cover-up. You had to intervene. Few things are black and white, and this is one of 'em. I think you did the right thing. But I also understand how you might feel like you fucked him over. Ask your heart: did you screw him to help him, or to get rid of him?"

Ida looked up at Ben with red eyes, sore cheeks, and quivering lips. She confessed, "To get rid of him. At the time, it was mostly about revenge, and teaching him a lesson."

Ben held her tight and said, "I love you so damn much. I never want to judge you. It sounds like he needed an intervention, or he could have really hurt someone."

"Sending him away had collateral damage. It affected his family in ways…." Ida clamed up in mid-sentence. There was so much more for her to elaborate on but the uneasiness to relive her past gave her pause and the fear of how Ben would react paralyzed her. Turning Ben off scared her to her bones.

"A drop in the ocean can cause a tidal wave. But it's not our fault if we didn't intend to make a tidal wave. I hope you see that," comforted Ben who himself was unsure what next to say. No everyone is as open as he was and he knew that and hence, chose not to press.

"I have this silly notion that one day I could confess it all to him, just to bury it, but he's nowhere to be found. I also really didn't try all that hard."

Ben gently clasped his palms on her sore cheeks and focused in on her swollen red eyes. "I know there's a strong, caring woman in there who gives a damn. She is who I am in love with. Just, should you ever feel the need to turn me in, let's talk about it first?"

Ida opened her mouth but then bit her lips. She was just not ready to risk everything that was building up by some attachments to her past. It tore at her inside as she kept her exterior intact. Her conflicted core promised to find a way to explain her complicated life to Ben – someday.

She looked at his handsome face and could not see past his big hazel eyes. He was so understanding, so supportive and the best listener she ever met. He always knew how to elicit a smile when she wasn't in the smiling mood. She nestled herself into his embrace and for a moment happily was lost in his heartbeat.

Chapter Fifteen

As late autumn descended on the city, the concrete jungle's sparsely scattered plant life rained golden, red, and yellow leaves and brittle branches. The weather gradually cooled, and the winter winds picked up. Sweater weather is snuggling weather.

For Ida and Ben, these weeks were filled with long lunches and even longer dinners, followed by cherished evening strolls against the most romantic backdrop. It's a shame to live in such a unique metropolis and not fully enjoy everything the Big Apple has to offer. And so, these two supercharged, enthralled lovers spent their time indulging in every bit of the fanfare that is New York City.

They hit renowned Broadway plays and off-Broadway hidden gems. They dined at street meat carts (they were brave), as well as five-star restaurants with every type of cuisine. Few cities in the world can offer delicacies from every nook and cranny of the globe. They particularly enjoyed diving headfirst into any hidden hole-in-the-wall that smelled absolutely scrumptious. At nearly every corner, a food truck of some sort tempted—most were tried, and some were regretted. But Ben and Ida didn't do it for the tasty nourishment; they did it for the company. Their whirlwind love had them deep diving into the liveliest city in the world.

New York is an eclectic masterpiece of historic sites, represented by literally every ethnic group on earth. Every religion, sociopolitical organization, cultural subsector, and artistic specialty is represented with breathtaking creativity. Museums and galleries seem to pop up unannounced, whether in the openness of Union Square, or in the famed galleries of SoHo, cutting edge artists of every sort showcase their talents, and they inspired Ben even more. Ida herself purchased several pieces to add a hint of her own taste to her cookie-cutter apartment and dull, standard office.

In the evenings they meandered down the pathways of Central Park, still buzzing with warmth despite the darker evenings and chillier winds. They were never lacking for words, but their strolls were usually silent and tranquil. It was as though a release valve had opened, and they could enjoy each other's company sharing a single thought and emotion. The park was their place to stop and breathe, but it wasn't theirs alone, as thousands of people relished the picturesque scene.

Fall in New York. Enough said.

Most nights ended the same way: back at her place, capping off the evening with either passionate lovemaking, or just falling into peaceful sleep in each other's arms. Neither one's sleep had ever been sounder.

Ben had scarcely been at his apartment, sometimes going days at a time without seeing home. Then, one day in late November, Ben stopped at his apartment to change clothes, pick up a few personal items, and head back out to meet Ida. When he opened the door, there was Buddy, sitting in his favorite recliner, seemingly fast asleep.

Suddenly Ben was overcome by guilt. He came to the shocking realization that he had neglected Buddy. He had moved in with the unsaid understanding that Buddy could use companionship in addition to help with basic household duties like as laundry, mail, groceries, and all-around tidiness. Sure, it was economically beneficial for Ben as well, but he had grown genuinely fond of the old-timer. Buddy had felt some inert obligation to care for him in return.

Ben's parents were like most parents, in love, with a balanced blend of agreements and disagreements, but they found middle ground often. By and large, he'd grown up in a modest, loving, small family unit. He never grew up wanting, except wishing for more time with his parents, or maybe a sibling to grow up with. Money had never been a highly prioritized goal, ever distant to seeking happiness. But his mother passed away when he was the tender age of eleven. She was the victim of an aggressive form of ovarian cancer. The loss devastated him. His father did his best to raise Ben thereafter, and by all accounts, he did just fine.

His father had been ten years older than his mother, and nearly fifty years separated father and son. At the age of sixty-nine, Ben's father suffered a sudden and massive heart attack at work. He had insisted on working, even at his age, as a maintenance man in a huge office building downtown. Ben had insisted that he could handle school and a part-time job, but his father had wanted to help.

After Ben was finally contacted, he arrived at the hospital hours too late, and only got to see his dad in the bereavement room. They had no other relatives in New York, and so only two of his dad's coworkers were there to comfort him. Ben sobbed the entire time, leaching tears onto his father's body until it was time to leave.

By nineteen, he was completely on his own. This shaped his independent mindset early on, as well as his ability to easily sympathize with those who struggle. Because of this, his first love had abused his extensive patience and latitude and his bottomless ability to care. It was of no true malicious intent, just immaturity's collateral damage, as is often the case for young lovers.

Buddy had helped fill that parental void, or maybe just a void in general. He amused Ben with his abrasive, sometimes politically incorrect humor and his wealth of firsthand history lessons, which spanned from his days in the military to his time working with pro-gressive political parties. Military action had sharpened Buddy's skeptical eye and fueled to change people's mindset. Then there was his knowledge of trivial information, and his expertise in comic books, antique toy collections, and pop culture fun facts. The icing on the cake was his far-fetched conspiracy theories, generally based more on unbelievable scope than anything rooted in credibility.

Now that Ida had brought joy to the innocent and talented young man who had been traumatized by the early death of his mother, the sudden death of his father, and a heartbreaking relationship with his ex-lover, he had rediscovered who he was meant to be at the cost of time spent with Buddy.

As Ben passed his roommate on the way to his room, Buddy coughed violently and suddenly woke up. Ben paused and asked aloud, "Buddy, are you okay, pal?"

After the coughing fit subsided, Buddy was silent. He issued no reply. He had his back to Ben, but his eyes were wide open and star-ing off into the other direction. Ben thought for a moment that Bud-dy would say something, but then he simply squeezed his eyes shut, pinched his lips together, and slipped back into sleep. Buddy was a proud chap. He would never admit to needing anyone or being lone-ly, no matter how true it may have been. He was a classic throwback, a hard ass personified, but he adjusted in his own way. His jovial na-ture, sometimes dirty and definitely R- rated, allowed him to accept some gloomy realities.

Ben entered his room in a state of self-reproach. He dropped his bag and sat on his bed. It felt like weeks since he had been here. He took out his phone and sat contemplatively motionless. As thoughts swirled about in his mind, Ben got up, gently shut his door, and made a phone call. He knew that the woman he had fallen in love with would understand his reconsideration and, moreover, be supportive of adjusting on the fly.

Minutes later, Ben emerged from his room with his jacket off and some new clothes on. He headed straight for the front closet and retrieved the vacuum, then plugged in the antique warhorse and gave it a go. It roared to life, sending Buddy into a surprised shriek.

"Christ almighty! You wanna give me a heart attack, do ya?"

Ben immediately turned off the vacuum and apologized.

Buddy exclaimed, "Jesus, Mary, and Joseph! I don't see ya for days, and when I do, you're either heading out, or heading in to head back out."

Ben nodded. "Yeah, I know. I've been tied up. My bad, Buddy."

"Your bad? Nah!" Buddy paused and took a self-loathing tone. "Don't apologize. You're a young, strong buck. You ain't supposed to be locked up in this house with an old fart like me. Besides, she must be one brick house mama jama, ain't she? That tail got you not knowin what direction you're goin? Hee hee! Am I right?"

Ben just laughed and declared, "You wouldn't dare say that if you met her."

"Guess you don't know me at all. I'd tell her straight to her face if she's a lady or a two-dollar—"

"Hey, now. Some respect, okay?"

Buddy quieted down, calmly keeping to himself, poorly suppressing his laughter.

Ben continued, "Well, you can tell her yourself what you think of her in a few hours."

"Come again?"

"She's coming over later. We're going to have dinner here. You'll finally meet her."

"Oh, you decided that, just like that?" Buddy sat up, offended and bewildered.

"Yup," Ben quipped, then continued vacuuming.

But Buddy motioned for Ben to turn it off. When the noise subsided, Buddy contested, "We can't. We just can't have that—" Buddy's reply was curtailed by another coughing fit.

Ben grew concerned. "Your cough is getting worse. You feeling all right?" Buddy waved him off as usual, then settled down. But Ben wouldn't let up. "Maybe I should cancel and take you down to the urgent care on Broadway."

Buddy finally returned, "No, not there. That's a last stop outfit, one hell of a shithole that place is. I'm fine. I need a cigarette, is all."

Ben was now adamant. "Okay, we can have dinner tonight on three conditions."

Buddy played along. "Oh, really! Let's hear 'em, Sir Williams!"

"Okay, first, you gotta be respectful. She means the world to me, so you better be on your best behavior, or no e-cigarette!"

Buddy squinted one eye in defiance. "I can do that. And two?"

"When was the last time you took a shower? Could you please, for the love of God, take one now, or at least douse yourself in your beloved Old Spice or something, because I'm not sure she'll make it through the doorway if you don't."

At first, Buddy took offense, but then he sniffed himself. "Fine. But I wanna make one thing crystal fucking clear: I'm doing it for her, okay? Not for you. Ya know, you should hole up with a squadron of twenty men in the heat and humidity of a goddamn tropical jungle for weeks! Then tell me what good smells like. Ha!"

"Great. While you take that much-needed shower, I'll perform a minor miracle and clean up this whole place."

After a momentary hesitation Buddy barked, "What's the third one!"

Ben inhaled. He tried his best to couch his words delicately. Buddy's health had always been a touchy subject, but after the coughing Ben felt compelled. "Tomorrow, I'm taking you down to the VA for a checkup."

Buddy slumped back in his recliner and calmly gathered his crutch. He struggled but made his way up from the chair on his own recognizance, and then looked Ben squarely in the eye. "I'm a perfect motherfucking gentleman. I'm going to powder myself now, and tomorrow I'm going to spend the entire day here in this chair, getting over the hangover, cause believe you me sonny, we are gonna drink tonight!"

Ben watched as the old man hobbled toward the bathroom singing "Two Out of Three Ain't Bad."

Moments later, the shower came to life, and Ben took a moment to smile.

Chapter Sixteen

At 8:30 that evening, three short knocks sounded at the apartment door. Ben was helping Buddy with his necktie, despite Ben suggesting that it was overkill. But Buddy had remained defiantly adamant. Rather than upset the miraculous applecart, he reassured Buddy that he looked perfect and smelled ravishing. When Buddy heard the knocks he playfully scolded, "Come now! It's not polite to leave a lady waiting."

Ben scowled at Buddy momentarily before sprinting for the door. When he opened it, there stood Ida in her immaculate beauty, wearing a spotless violet overcoat and a chic, floppy black hat. A few dark strands framed her gorgeous face. She was elegant and stunning, as always. She never wore too much makeup or bathed in overpowering perfume. She wasn't excessive in anything she did. She was perfect.

She held a colorful bouquet in one hand and struggled with a large brown grocery bag in the other. They kissed, then embraced. Ben didn't even try to curtail their passionate greeting— until it was interrupted by Buddy's increasingly concerning cough. Buddy pardoned himself, then hobbled into the living room, aided by his one crutch. He cordially welcomed Ida into their humble abode, and Ben reminded himself to make sure Buddy made good on his hospital promise.

Truly, Ben had pulled off the minor miracle. Within three short hours (and four garbage bags), the unkempt apartment was tidied, streamlined, and presentable. Most of the counters, as well as the appliances and even some of the visible walls, were clean and shiny, though there were some spots that would only be remedied by a paint job. The vacuum closet was packed tight with laundry bags and a deodorizer gel. The faint lemon scent of disinfectant undercut the domicile, though Ben had opened the windows to air the place out, letting in the cool evening air. Cleverly, he had something appetizing baking in the oven, which also helped to undercut the sanitizers.

Ida stabbed at a guess. "Is that apple pie I smell? Or roast pork?"

Buddy was impressed. "My, this young lady has quite the nose! Actually, it's both."

"Well, not roast pork with apple strudel stuffing, but close!" said Ben.

Buddy said, "I admit, it's the grocery's finest apple pie. I can't bake a lick, I promise you, but you'll be licking your fingers clean! It's absolutely scrumptious! Like Ben here. I'm sure you can pick him clean, bone dry!"

Ben intensified his stare at Buddy, trying to remind him of his manners and his promise of PG-rated conversation—which Buddy had already ignored. Not even three minutes had elapsed, and the door for crude comments had been flung wide open.

But Ida surprised Ben and teased back, "Oh, how randy of you! Well then, I might forgo dinner in order to sink my teeth into two desserts."

Ben was doubly shocked. A discreet wink from Ida assured him that she would be a sport and play along. After all, she had been fore-warned about Buddy—several times. Ben grinned back, brimming with appreciation as Ida continued to banter with his roommate. Buddy, meanwhile, had turned beet red with giddiness, rejuvenated by conversation with someone other than Ben or himself or the television. He was beside himself now.

Ida remarked, "You know, Ben talks about you often, and so fondly."

"He talks about me? All good, I hope," feared Buddy.

"Oh, terribly good things, I'm afraid. Honestly, it's quite nauseating, so I was absolutely determined to find out about you for myself."

"Well, he's a great kid."

Ida beamed at Ben and agreed with a twinkle in her eye. "Oh, indeed he is." She gently laid her fingers on Buddy's shoulder and said with admiration, "So, I hear you're a service veteran. We all owe a great debt to you for keeping the world safe."

And then Buddy really began to appreciate this lady's beauty, charm, and grace. He began to curb his potty mouth and engaged in adult, civil conversation—while of course still maintaining his edge.

He reprehensibly motioned to Ben with a bit of tongue in cheek. "Come, now! What kind of gentleman are you to not take this fine lady's coat? And give her a tour of the castle, why don't cha."

Ben and Ida exchanged amused smiles. Earlier, on the phone, he had apologized. Initially, he was going to cancel their dinner plans, but then he was suddenly struck by the ingenious idea to share a dinner, just the three of them. That way, Buddy would finally understand the reason for Ben's notable absence. Of course, he worried that Buddy's rough joking and caustic sense of humor might make for a regrettable evening, but he felt compelled to explain himself through the best body of evidence he could find.

Ida, on the other hand, had been terrified that his phone call was the beginning of the end. She had a deep-rooted fear of Ben suddenly growing bored of her. So, as Ben had unraveled his modification of dinner plans, Ida was choking back tears, trying to maintain normal breathing and heart rate—but then she was touched. Beyond flattered. This was basically an introduction to the closest family he had. She had no such counterpart, not in the States, at least, and even if they were to venture back to England, her family was not exactly close. Her father was estranged, and her mother was cold, distant, and not much of a conversationalist—more of a critic.

She knew Ben had a good heart, but his appreciation for Buddy had proved that he was a good man. He was special. He cared so much for his friend that he knew the small, gracious act of inclusion would mean a lot to him. This was family time, and it was genuine, and she was family as well.

Buddy's robust personality was on full display. So was the noticeably hacking cough. Several times during the evening, Ida asked if Buddy was all right or needed assistance. Every time, Buddy just joked that it was old age, that this was his new norm. Besides that, the evening was a smashing success. Buddy's growing estrangement was relieved, and Ida's deeper inclusion into Ben's world was even more fulfilling than she had imagined. As for Ben, he never knew that pairing Ida and Buddy would mean so much to them, or to himself. It surprised him how well the two hit it off, but it had done wonders for the three of them. This was his evolving world, with the two people who meant the most to him.

Ida helped Ben clean up. She brought trash and dishes and cups into the kitchen. Ben was ever so appreciative, but before he could utter a word, he was pitted against the wall. Ida had taken this moment to aggressively kiss and fondle Ben, whispering in between labored breaths, "I've never wanted you more!"

They continued for what seemed like an eternity. By the time they were done, Ben was flushed; his blood flooded red hot through every pulsating vessel, and the passion reverberated every nerve. Ida, too, was burning with desire, overcome by lust. Her chest heaved like a starved lioness going in for the kill.

Ben held her and paused the foreplay. "Was it the apple pie? Cause then, like, I'm buyin the whole shelf, every goddamn box?"

Ida playfully slapped at him. "Of course not, silly! It was edible, but, please, standards." After composing herself, she got serious. "You seem to outdo yourself at every turn. I suspect you aren't even aware of how naturally and effortlessly you make everyone around you feel better, about themselves, about life, about what matters. You're like a walking serenity prayer."

Ben was flattered, and at the same time lost for words.

Ida continued, "I fall deeper and deeper into you each day, Mr. Benito Emilio Williams. I am beyond fortunate that you walked into my life. Like tonight. What you did for Buddy was really thoughtful. You bridged the people in your life who are special to you, and that means so much to us both. I hope you see that!"

"No biggie. It was a judgment call, really. I saw the loneliness in his eyes, and I wanted to help. I'm just so glad you were down for it too."

Ida took in a deep, prepared breath and said, "I confess, when I heard your plan, I feared you may have gotten bored of us, and decided to make up some excuse to bail. But as your idea took shape, I saw that I could not have been more wrong! You are a rare bird, indeed."

Ben winced and shook his head, then took hold of Ida's hands and drew her near. "I am never bored with us. Every day I look forward to hearing your voice, your wit, anything you have to say. I fear one day it might be me who does not live up to your standards. I may not be worthy of what you envision."

Ida was abhorred by the thought. "How could you even think that!?"

Ben tried to hide his shame. "Look, I barely hold down two part-time jobs. I split rent with a disabled vet. I don't have a dime to my name. I haven't published anything, anywhere. I'm not exactly lighting the world on fire over here."

Ida was dumbfounded. Ben, still holding Ida's hands, paused to choose his words with clarity and then continued, "Since meeting you, I find myself a crossroads. I want to *be* more, because I want to stay with you. And I can't keep doing what I've been doing. I gotta shake things up. Trust me, I've given this a lot of thought."

"I'm not certain I understand what you're saying."

"Work's gotta change. My end goal, to be a writer, has to change. I spend most nights at your place, and if we keep moving in this direction, I'm not about to mooch off of you. I don't do that. I pull my weight."

"I know that," said Ida. "Even a blind man could see that. You are without a doubt one of the most responsible and considerate people walking the earth."

All of a sudden there was awkward silence between them. They had been riding this wave of euphoria they never talked about their relationship and what direction it should go. They were both lost in thought and both even more afraid to further the conversation. Neither was ready for this right now this fast. The lighthearted evening had taken an abrupt left turn.

Ida eventually said, "What can I do to help you realize your goals?" Silently, she feared some measure of distance was coming. Her one emotional relationship weighed on her like a ten-ton anchor. But she could not resist, and added, "And what does this mean for us?"

Ben took his time before responding, then said slowly, "The goal is to be us, but stronger. I want to be a person you can count on and be proud of. You've given me a jolt, and—"

Ida's cell phone was suddenly ringing. She glanced at the caller ID and crumpled her eyebrows, perplexed, then let it ring through to voicemail. Ben used the opportunity to gather his thoughts. If he was going to dedicate more time to writing, it would mean less time at the bookstore and less time with Ida.

In his memory bank, Ben found the snippets of his speech that he had been rehearsing. He wanted to lay out his plan for more free time to write and more quality time with her, but it may mean less frequency. Just as he was about to launch into it, Ida's phone rang again. This time, before the second ring, she excused herself. "Sorry, I have to take this." And in expeditious fashion, Ida glided to the living room, eased open the door and continued the phone call in the hallway.

Ben stood blinking, wondering what had just happened. He had some serious thoughts about their relationship and his immediate future. He'd had a knot in his stomach for a while now, worried about how to bring up this topic and afraid of how Ida would respond. She had been supportive of his writing from the outset. She never kept tabs on who paid, or seemed to notice any money matters. By the same token, Ben had always been self-sufficient, and proud of it. He was not about to lounge around her apartment, use her debit card, and live life with a benefactor. He could not dream of it. But how could he have his cake and eat it too?

The evening had gone so well. He had successfully merged the two largest components of his life in a smashing, entertaining evening. Ida and Buddy seemed to genuinely like each other. Shocking! But now she got a call and whizzed off into the hallway, just when his anxiety had risen to an all-time high.

Ben's blinking was a sure onset of an anxiety attack. Next would come some escalating hyperventilation and tightening of his chest.

Beads of sweat would follow, trickling down his temples, which would be throbbing by then. Quick breaths would thin his oxygen supply, as if he were sprinting up a hill, and his mind would be racing around a NASCAR track at a thousand miles an hour. The lightheaded dizziness that followed would cause Ben to take a seat and center himself.

That was his life pre-Ida, and now he felt the demons of anxiety creep up to his new, steady self. He took a few calming breaths, exercises Dr. Hoda had suggested. He thought about the bottle of benzodiazepine back on his dresser, the antianxiety pills she had prescribed. Though he still had an overdeveloped fear of addiction, he had to wonder whether or not they would have helped in this moment.

With Ida in his life, Ben had not had anything close to a full-blown panic attack.

Fortunately, Buddy entered the kitchen and noticed Ben frozen in thought, fighting his angst and calming himself with meditative breaths. When Buddy looked around and noticed Ida wasn't there, he glanced back at Ben and cracked, "Oh, come on! The apple pie wasn't that bad, was it?"

Chapter Seventeen

The mood in New York City is unique due to its size, history, and technical wonders. In the wintry nights of Christmastime, beautifully lit trees illuminate the festive city blocks. Carols blare from cleverly disguised decorations. The sidewalks are lined with vendors selling everything from reprint photos to scarves, mittens, and hats, from novelty seasonal gifts and ornaments to cell phone accessories. Who can say they haven't purchased an "I Love NY" souvenir or a Statue of Liberty foam finger? The aromas of roasted chestnuts, peanuts, hot apple cider, hot chocolate, and pastries fill the air this time of year. The scent of pine with an undercurrent of peppermint permeates the air. When it comes right down to it, Christmas in New York is an experience worth taking in.

The evening before New Year's Eve, Ben and Ida met up with Meck and Arty for happy hour. They consumed a few cocktails at a local pub, then spontaneously decided to ice skate in Bryant Park. The last scatterings of autumn leaves had disappeared weeks ago, and barren trees lined the sidewalks. People had transitioned from light jackets and sweaters into some sort of warmer winter covering. Hats and gloves, down jackets, and wool overcoats hurried to and fro, desperately seeking refuge from the cold.

Darkness fell at 4:30 p.m. As twilight bridged the gap to evening, sparkling white lights with bluish hues outlined nearly every tree. Bryant Park is nestled just south of the hustle and bustle of Times Square and is no stranger to tourist fanfare. It's surrounded by impressive gothic architecture, but some modern, glass-wrapped skyscrapers have begun to encroach. Still, it is a welcome reprieve from the concrete jungle.

For Ben and Ida, ice skating in the center rink was the call of the wild du jour. Ben had not ice skated a day in his life. Meanwhile, unbeknownst to him, Ida had spent many of her formidable years in competitive skating. Her grandmother had been positively sure that Ida was the next Michelle Kwan. She had spent endless days and weekends in expensive practice time with private instructors, repeating move after move, falling on rock hard ice, hopelessly alone with a stern and unforgiving coach. In the beginning, she'd appreciated the time with her Filipino grandmother. Lola Esther was love personified.

Ida repeatedly placed, and even won a few championships. But the all-too-familiar sadness of only one parent showing up dampened any victory. They'd split when she was just three years old. The divorce was acrimonious, bitter, and drawn out over several years. Her parents always bickered about money, but Ida never had one destitute day—though she'd have traded all her lavish things for an unassuming, loving home. As time went on, and her grandmother's health worsened, ice skating became impractical. It just wasn't the same. It had lost its luster, and Ida eventually replaced it with academics and other pursuits.

Back in the pub, when the suggestion to ice skate first came about, Ida hadn't known exactly how to respond. It was Ben who had impulsively thrown it out there, perhaps after the third mixed drink. Initially, Ida was resistant. She had buried the memories of her childhood a long time ago. But, in the flow of the moment, she acquiesced, especially since the rink was right in front of them out the pub window.

As they donned the ice skates, Ben asked, "Have you ever skated before?"

Ida returned, "Quite a bit, actually, when I was a tot. But it's been years. Another lifetime if you will. Yourself?"

Ben smiled and replied, "Not a day in my life. So don't laugh too hard."

Ida smiled, sincerely amused by Ben's impulsiveness and boyish confidence.

The moment they got on the ice, Ben slipped and fell, rather hard. In true Ben fashion, he laughed off his embarrassment. "Holy shit! This is insane. Everyone makes it seem way easy!"

Ida calmed him with a smile. "Take my hand."

Without hesitation, Ben reached for Ida's extended hand. She reassured him. "This is quite possibly the most unnatural thing to do with your legs, besides cycling, and I assume you can ride a bicycle?"

Ben nodded, bewildered. "This ain't nothing like riding a bike." Yet Ben seemed completely secure in her hands.

Ida continued, "As long as you find your balance, you can ice skate. And you are all about balance, my dear."

She started out with baby steps, as though they were learning to walk. Slowly but surely, despite a few falls, Ben made great strides in moving about the ice. The two were once again locked in their own enchanted world. It was as though no one else existed. They chiseled at the ice, milling around the crowded rink for about an hour. With the festive music, the seasonal aromas, and the bright moonlight, Ida and Ben were nestled in each other's arms in joyful cold—and sometimes painful falls.

After gathering Ben up off the ice one final time, the two lovers found a relatively empty spot near the side rail and kissed. Their cracked lips found moisture as exhilarating warmth shot down their bodies. The rush brought heat to their frigid cheeks. Few romantic moments got such a perfect setting. It would remain a timeless memory for each of them.

Ben said, "I have never been in love like I am right now."

Ida gazed into Ben's eyes and responded, "I am so in love with you, and I don't want anything to ever end this night."

They kissed again, releasing steam into the frigid night air. Just like when they first met, all background sights and sounds dissipated. The two lovers embraced as though they were the only two at Bryant Park. For all intents and purposes, they were.

Afterward, exhausted, bruised, and battered enough, they skated off the ice and warmed up with hot cocoa with whipped cream. The two sat in peaceful silence sipping the piping hot, delicious beverages.

Ida broke the silence, recounting her childhood ice skating lessons and her bond with her grandmother. She did not often talk about her past in detail, but now, she spoke in a resolute tone.

Hearing about her parents' unhappy marriage broke Ben's heart. "I'm so sorry you had to go through all that," he said.

Ida gulped down her drink, then said, "There have been worse childhoods. I never wanted for anything, except what others had: siblings, a two-parent household, large family gatherings. You know that sort of stuff."

Ben said, "I wanted siblings too. I suppose we make do in different ways. Like, well, I had an imaginary friend, Lukas. He was my spin on the Marvel crime fighter Luke Cage. We'd go on vigilante-type missions and combat the mean streets of this city together, looking to put away the bad guys. But I feel for ya. We never had a lot, but we had each other. I remember when my mom was still alive, how much my parents genuinely loved each other. I knew I always wanted that."

Ida pinched his cheek affectionately and smiled. "That's one of the many wondrous parts of you. You know what's important, what matters. You make me feel that way all the time, like I'm the only one in the room and everything else is just fluff."

Ben smiled back. "It only works when you take what I give and return it tenfold."

They stretched over the small café table and kissed. The evening was absolutely perfect—until Meck and Arty reappeared. Arty held a mistletoe bundle over their heads. He had apparently stolen it from some decorative window dressing. Ida was genuinely amused, but Ben grew irritated at Arty's immature behavior.

Ida, always of sound intuition, sensed that the boys needed time to be boys. She knew Ben hadn't really had time to hang out with his friends and just let loose. In her heart, she knew their time together was tender and special, but everyone—including her—needed me-time. Nothing was worse than in her previous relationship, where they had been defined as A Couple. If she showed up to an event without Spencer, everyone would be in an uproar. They had been defined as Idalis-and-Spencer, a unit. It was, in her eyes, pathetic.

Ironically, being seen as a couple had made her feel lonelier, like a half-defined person. By the end of that relationship, she'd realized that it was of the utmost importance to be who *she* wanted to be, first and foremost. In leaving Spencer, she'd wanted to redefine who she really was. But this took more time than she had expected. She was still searching, still unsatisfied.

Was she slipping into the same old habit of being defined by her relationship? Were they Ida-and-Ben?

After a few rounds, Ida diplomatically excused herself, citing tons of boring paperwork and meetings for her the next day. She insisted that Ben and his buddies have an enjoyable and safe stag night out. Ida warned Meck and Arty, the two misfits, to behave. Should any harm fall onto Ben, she would hold them personally responsible, and there would be hell's full price to pay.

The two boys found it rather amusing and played along. They seemed eager to hang out with their friend, whose free time had mostly been consumed by Ida. In truth, they knew just how lucky Ben was.

But this was a night for the boys.

Ida grabbed Ben and danced until they were in the center of the bar and, in full view of everyone, kissed and slobbered all over him, clutching his tight, well-defined derriere. Then she whispered into his ear, "I love you. Have fun and try not to land in jail with these two when you have a perfectly warm bed waiting for you. I'll be wearing nothing under the covers. Feel free to wake me when you come home."

Ben argued, "Screw these two barbarians! I'm coming home with you now!"

But Ida remained stoic. "No! You should hang out a bit. Boys need to be boys." She pecked him on the nose and smiled. "Have a smashing, grand time."

Ben tracked her out the door until she was beyond sight.

Arty horse-collared Ben playfully and teased, "Why am I always lapping you, lover boy? Come on, we got a pint with your name on it!"

Chapter Eighteen

The next morning, Ida cheerfully trotted toward her office. She had some extra pep in her step and a make-no-mistake-about-it smile. She wore her usual oversized sunglasses and her trendy sheer scarf. Her strut echoed its usual demonstrative sharp tap, but she was blissfully at ease.

Everyone in the office had noticed. She was definitely the buzz around the watercooler—or, more precisely, around the text message chains. Carmen had experienced the change up close and personal. She was at the receiving end of Ida's casual conversations, which spanned from fashion, to dinner hot spots, and even to her own personal life. Ida had opened up exponentially, taking time to ask about Carmen's personal life and engage in real conversations, not just the obligatory, mindless office chitchat.

Yes, Ida had transformed into a quasi-approachable manager—although most of the minions still hesitated to get too close. They didn't dare ask her about her personal life. But she was more pleasant to deal with without the looming threat of having their livelihood dissolved in a snap.

She opened her door, tossed her sunglasses and scarf aside, and hung her cashmere overcoat. As usual, she fingered through rows of Post-it messages on her computer screen. One note in particular caused her to pause. She had to reread it over and over again. Her mouth grew parched, and her eyes reflected stunned disbelief. She reached for her desk phone and dialed #2 on her speed dial.

Carmen picked up. "Yes, Ms. Shah?"

Ida was couching her words. "Ah, that Post-it note from this morning, the one marked urgent?"

"Yes, Ms. Shah?"

"When did you get that message?"

"Let me review the voicemail, ma'am."

"Oh, it was a voicemail?"

"Yes."

"Okay. Please do so and let me know."

"Absolutely, Ms. Shah."

Ida hung up, then immediately shuffled through her pocketbook, finally locating her cell phone. She rushed to unlock her it, then scrolled through her notifications—no missed calls, and no voicemails. She stared off at the distant wall, panicked.

The office phone rang, startling her. She picked it up. "Yes, Carmen?"

"Ms. Shah, the call was time-stamped at two thirty-five."

"Two thirty-five am?" Ida was stunned.

"Yes, ma'am."

"Okay. Thank you."

Ida hung up the phone, then searched for what to do next. She dialed Ben's number, silently begging for him to pick up. Oddly enough, the call went straight to voicemail. She was flummoxed. She had met Ben's friends, Meck and Arty, on many occasions and of course Buddy, but she didn't have anyone's contact information. Ben's apartment was too far for a taxi during the snail's pace of morning rush hour traffic, which in New York is a contradiction in terms. But she had to get to him soon. A flash of genius graced her brain, and she grabbed her scarf and sunglasses, threw on her overcoat back on, and bolted out of her office. She frantically backtracked to Carmen's desk. "Carmen, I have a family emergency. Hold all my calls! Or, rather, forward them to my cell. I won't be in for the rest of the day, and let's leave it at that for now."

Carmen dared to ask, "Ms. Shah, is everything all right?"

Ida shouted back as she dashed for the elevator, "Yes! No. I don't know." She swooped into the elevator, leaving Carmen in stunned silence.

Minutes later, Ida barged into the Abbey May Bookstore. Pearl straightened up from behind her book and noticed an unusually frazzled Ida making a beeline toward her.

Ida managed to calm herself before speaking. "Pearl, is it?"

Pearl nodded. "Ida?"

Ida closed her eyes and nodded. "Yes. I'm in a bit of a pickle, and I desperately need your assistance. Will you help me?"

Pearl nodded again, looking very eager. "Sure, what's up?"

Ida inhaled. Between her office door and the bookstore, she'd rehearsed her plea at least a hundred times. From the way Ben had described Pearl, she was the last person on earth Ida would ask for help. Her constant flirtations weren't threatening so much as annoying. But Ida was at her wit's end when she pleaded, "Someone I know had just a horrific car accident. I must see to their condition straight away."

Pearl cried, "Holy shit!"

"Holy shit is right! I have to go immediately. I've been trying to get in contact with Ben, but his phone is going directly to voicemail. I texted him but haven't received a reply. He was out with Meck and Arty last night. Do you know them, or their phone numbers?"

"Oh, those two losers. Yeah, if there ever was a pair that couldn't hold their liquor, it's those two. Meck, that guy thinks he's the world's greatest singer, and greatest lover. I mean, he can karaoke some songs, but then he reaches and..." She shook her head in disapproval.

"I know, boys will be boys. Do you have either one of their numbers?"

Pearl shook her head with an insincere, transparent look of concern.

Ida eyed a legal pad on Pearl's desk and reached for it. "Might I leave him a note?"

"Ah, yeah. Sure," huffed Pearl. Ida had already begun writing.

She fought the urge to be upset with Ben. The unraveling situation wasn't his fault. After all, it was she who insisted Ben spend time with his friends. This was just a most inopportune series of events. She had learned a long time ago when composing e-mails and writing notes to leave emotions out.

Pearl added, "He should be in for the noon shift. Hopefully he'll have recovered by then." She watched with curiosity tempered with restraint, not wanting to appear nosy.

Ida folded the paper neatly and handed it to Pearl. "Would you see to it that Ben gets this as soon as possible?"

Pearl took the note and nodded with a forced smile. "Absolutely."

"Thanks so much. I really have to run now. And thank you again, wholeheartedly."

"Don't mention it. Please."

Ida took a brief moment to process a response. An explosion of emotions and thoughts was running through her head—clarity was not her friend right now. She cursed herself for the predicament she found herself in.

Pearl watched as Ida mimicked the *The Thinker*, deep in thought. After some deliberation, she finally bid farewell. "I should go now. I do appreciate this. Thanks so much."

Pearl said, "Take care."

She waited a full five minutes before she unfolded Ida's note behind the cover of her book.

After she finished reading, she said to herself, "How interesting, Ms. Fancy Pants."

Chapter Nineteen

That same morning—or, more accurately, mid-morning—Ben shuffled toward the bathroom at Meck and Arty's place. He blindly felt his way to the toilet and relieved himself, hoping most of it made it to the target. He held himself upright by palming the tiled wall. This helped him fight the urge to vomit. If he'd been at home, he'd have expelled the vile liquids and felt much better. Thankfully, plentiful glasses of water had helped retard the caustic eruption. Ben was never much for drinking. A few beers or a single glass of wine would normally suffice. Truth be told, he preferred a great cup of coffee, or an iced tea. But the night had been fabulous, and long past due. It began as a simply magical evening on the ice with the love of his life, and then with his two best buds. Still, he could do without the body aches. Whether they were from the ice rink or the booze, it was too early to say.

He'd fallen asleep feeling great, on top of the world. Friends and lovers do that; they heighten the mood and make for memorable, joyous evenings. He couldn't remember ever feeling this festive. A kaleidoscope of fond memories swirled about in his dizzy head. He had come a long way since that afternoon at Comic Con when he ditched his friends and set his cell phone to silent. Then it occurred to him. His cell phone. Where was it? He was supposed to end up at Ida's apartment— 'home' as she referenced it. He was supposed to wake her up. She'd be naked and receptive. The bed would be warm and inviting and oh-so-comforting.

Indeed, after 1:00 a.m., everything was a blur. Except for the copious amounts of water he'd downed in a desperate attempt to remain on the sober side of drunk, he could only remember following Meck and Arty around like a simpleton sheep. Somehow, he'd ended up on their raggedy sofa instead of under the intimate red satin sheets of Ida's bed. Ben quickly pulled up his pants, then drank straight from the sink faucet, taking gulps at a time, nearly choking.

Afterward, he closed his eyes and steadied himself against the room, which had started to spin. He tried to retrace his steps, but the pounding headache just wouldn't let him. Slowly, he walked over to the sofa and knifed his hands around the pillows in search of his cell phone. Horrified by some of the identified and unidentified objects that met his hand, he forged onward, grasping at old gum, candy wrappers, loose change, a pen, and other undesirables. Some items were fuzzy, some were slimy, and a few he swore may have bitten him. His thoughts became clearer but still showed up in fragments. He walked the perimeter of the sofa and finally spotted his jacket, tucked away where the far wall met the floor. Frantically, he turned every pocket inside out. He was relieved to find his money clip and the few dollars it contained, plus his keys and a few receipts, but nothing else. No phone.

Ben rubbed his forehead, trying to soothe the brain throb. He needed to think. He pulled at his thick bushy hair, trying to reconstruct last night's steps. At the end of the coffee table was Meck's phone. Ben knew the security code would be 6666, as Meck always boasted that he was extra evil. He focused intensely to recall his own number before realizing he most surely was listed in Meck's contacts. He cringed at the photo associated with his name: a photo from years ago, when he had dressed up as Cinderella on a dare.

But there was no time to dwell on that now. He took note of the present time—10:35 a.m.—and called his own number. His head hurt more with every self-deprecating curse. He had to be at the bookstore by noon for his shift. He was dumbfounded by how long he had been knocked out.

"Shit!" yelled Ben as the call went straight to voicemail, a sure sign the battery had died. It seemed unlikely that he would find his phone now. He searched the doorway, and under the coffee table, and he upended every piece of junk littering the pigsty of a bachelor pad. There were magazines scattered about, and half empty pizza boxes from what could have been weeks ago, along with sandwich wrappers and beer cans that were not so empty. He wondered how there weren't any roaches or rodents—though he quickly and repulsively saw there were. The seasonal, aromatic scent of Bryant Park was a distant mystery as the rotting stench blended with stale beer and triggered a reflex—Ben dashed for the toilet and unleashed the night's debauchery into the bowl. His bedtime water came rushing out with everything else, in full demonic exorcist style.

Ben fell to his knees, laboring to breathe, hands on the seat. He was in a yoga praying position, begging the hangover gods for mercy. He reached out to flush the toilet, then brought it back to expel some more. The last few heaves were basically residual reactions, the painful, gagging, dry variety. Now his head started to pulsate, and the room began to dilate and contract. As he struggled to stand up, he began to feel as if he were riding tsunami waves. When he knelt back down to close his eyes and refocus, recenter, and get a grip, his midline burned and strained.

He wasn't used to all-night benders, but he'd been in a celebratory mood, and now he was paying the price. He remained bent over the bowl for a while, concentrating on slowing his breathing and clearing his head. The quiet morning was no small favor.

Then Meck's deep, resonating voice cracked an unwelcome comment: "It's a damn shame when a man can't hold his liquor."

Ben barely opened one eyelid, catching a fuzzy glimpse of Meck as he stood in his gray sweatpants and ugly Christmas sweater. He slowly shook his head, shrugged his shoulders, and crossed his arms.

With his last bit of strength, Ben raised his arm and flicked up his middle finger. Meck chuckled his deep, cavernous laugh, then proceeded to help Ben off the floor. Being of massive size and strength, it was easy for Meck to lift Ben up, although Ben begged for Meck to be as gentle as he could. But Meck was anything but gentle. Eventually, he plopped Ben on the sofa and prodded, "Damn, bro. That's weak. Good thing your little boo went home and didn't watch you get wrecked."

Ben gathered himself as best he could. Still with his eyes closed and cradling a throw pillow, he contested, "I was good until I got grossed out by all the nasty pizza boxes and food wrappers and shit! There's rats and maggots and all sorts of gnarly smells in this place. It should be condemned, man."

"Condemned? Man, you the fool who should be condemned. You didn't hold down a goddamn thing. Everything from the pits of hell was yakked up in there! I saw the whole damn sorry mess. Made most of it in the can! I'm actually impressed. I'll give you props for that, at least."

Ben insisted, "Dude, take a look under this sofa right here. You're breeding botulin down here!"

Meck huffed but bent down to take a look. He scanned the debris and squinted in agreement. "Ain't no thing."

"You need to slash and burn this place! Salt the earth!"

"Okay, slow your roll, partner. I'll let that slide cause it's the yack talkin! Why you lookin all up under there, anyways?"

Ben suddenly remembered why, and his eyes popped open. "My cell! I think I lost it last night. I was looking all over for it. Couldn't find it. Then I grabbed your phone and called it. Straight to voicemail."

"You used my phone? So not cool, bro. How the hell did you unlock it?"

Ben dropped his head in disbelief. "Really, man? You go around boasting how extra evil you are!"

"So?"

"Six, six, six, plus six? Extra evil?"

Meck looked amazed. He was truly shocked that Ben had figured him out.

But Ben was focused on the issue at hand. "Look, I must have dropped it at the bar last night. Did we go anywhere else after that?"

Meck shot Ben a look of stunned disbelief and cautiously asked, "You don't remember anything, do you?"

Ben searched his mind but feared the worst. "Oh, man, no. Nothing after the bar. I remember singing a couple of tunes. Then I downed all those glasses of water. And then I woke up here."

"Shoot! First off, that wasn't water. It was tequila. Your tongue must have been so numb, couldn't tell the difference."

"You ordered me glasses of tequila?"

"So, I guess you don't remember the bachelorette party coming in, all dressed in skimpy red Santa's little helper outfits?"

"No!"

"The one hot redhead girl dancing with you?"

"No!"

"Then the striptease? The one you put on?"

"Hell no!"

"Not even the drinking games?"

"Oh, God no!

"How about the guy you called a midget, with his girl right there, right fucking there?"

"No! I would never!"

"Blame it on the alcohol, I guess."

"Why would I say that?"

"They weren't even that small—not that it's excusable under any circumstances."

"Says the six-foot-five behemoth who calls everyone fun-sized."

"Hey, this ain't about me, bro. I can handle my shit."

Ben clasped his hands to his cheeks in utter anguish. Just then, Arty emerged from his room and headed straight for the bathroom. He stopped short of the toilet, noticed the mess, and smelled the sour stench of regurgitation. Then he remarked, "Ben, nothing is worse than a man who can't hold his liquor."

Ben wailed in disgust. Meck joined Arty at the bathroom door as they ogled at the wreck that was Ben.

Ben finally looked at Arty and apologized. "Man, I'm sorry for all the shit I said last night, with the stripping and the midget and the singing and whatever else."

Arty seemed perplexed. "What the hell are you talking about? After the tequila, you passed out. We sat you down in the corner somewhere. After a while the bartender started to play sheriff, so we had to bounce. We threw you in a cab and headed back here. You babbled on and on about Ida and being dropped off at her place. But, dude, you were in no condition to be around a pretty woman like that. We saved you from total embarrassment."

Ben suddenly froze. "What. You mean I didn't do anything stupid?"

Arty shrugged. "Other than drink like a lightweight freshman at a keg party? No. All you did was end a boys' night out early—too damn early. We kicked back and watched *Miracle on 34th Street* until it bored us to sleep."

"What!" shouted Ben.

"Well, I think a thank-you is in order!" remarked Arty.

Ben jumped up and charged at Meck, whaling away at his body in a feeble attempt to hurt him. Meck simply laughed louder and heartier. As Ben's tirade died down and Meck's laughter dissipated, he picked Ben up and gently tossed him back onto the sofa. "Just sleep it off, bro. And fix your face, while you're at it. We're just messin with you!"

Arty put on the coffee. Ben started to clean up the bathroom. Finding paper towels and cleaning products was a challenge, so he eventually used toilet paper and shampoo and did the best he could.

Ben realized that it was now 11:30 a.m. "Great, I'm gonna be late for work now!"

Meck said, "Chillax bro! You getting into Bonkers Ben mode! Look, I'll call the bar and check on your phone. Arty, let Ben use your phone to call the bookstore. Just say you ate something that didn't agree with you. Or just straight call out!"

Ben was processing information at a delayed rate. Meck's plan of action seemed perfect. After all, Meck was an expert at getting out of work. He finally got in contact with the bar manager, who confirmed that a few phones had been recovered last night—the description matched one.

When Pearl picked up the phone, she laid into him. "Ben, where the hell are you? You sound wrecked as hell!"

Ben fumbled over his words. "Yes. I mean, no. I ate something that didn't—"

"Save it."

"My phone died."

"Yeah, yeah, yeah. Save it for—"

"Did Ida call looking for me?"

A stretch of concerning silence filled the dead air. Pearl eventually responded in a resounding, "Nope!"

Ben persisted, "You sure? Cause she's called before, and sometimes I don't get the message…."

Pearl responded instantaneously, "What's it worth to ya if she did?"

"Stop screwing me, Pearl!"

"You know, it's so sad how wrapped around that stuck-up bitch's finger you are. So fucking sad, loser!"

"Pearl?"

"Don't worry, if she calls, I'll just let her know you're having breakfast with your other hooch!" Pearl then hung up, further infuriating Ben. He threw the phone on the sofa and it subsequently bounced onto the floor.

"Yo! The phone, bro!"

"Sorry. This shitstorm is getting worse and worse."

Meck and Arty stood in silence, as even these glorified primates knew things were getting tense, and in matters of relationships, it's best to stay out of it.

Meck suggested, "Look you gotta go downtown anyway to get your phone, right? After you get it, head to the bookstore and see what's up."

Once again Meck's level-headedness shined through.

Ben sarcastically sniped, "This day is getting better and better."

Meck again offered his phone to Ben. "Yo, you might wanna hit up your girl?"

Ben, exasperated and defeated, said, "I would, but I don't know her number by heart. I'm so screwed. I gotta get my cell."

Chapter Twenty

After retrieving his dead phone from the bar, Ben sprinted nearly twenty city blocks, arriving at the Abbey May Bookstore deeply out of breath. He barged through the front doors, starling the browsing patrons. Pearl placed her book down with contempt and motioned for Ben to come toward her.

She hissed, "Jesus H. Christ! You look like hell chewed you up and shitted you out!"

Ben waited to catch his breath and then said, "Look, I'm trashed. I know."

"Clearly."

"I puked my brains out all morning, and I lost my phone last night. I just got it back, but it's as dead as your social life."

"Well, you know what, to hell with you, you fucking asshole!"

Ben growled, "Pearl! I'm having a bad day, a really bad day. I'm sorry. It was a bad joke. I'm a hot mess, and I'm sorry."

Pearl was a piping hot volcano. She kept her eyes fixed on her book while Ben remained standing, dazed and bewildered like a lost child. Pearl eventually looked sideways at Ben before breaking her silence, "So, got trashed a bit early? New Year's Eve is tonight, genius."

Ben shook his head, full of self-loathing, then lamented, "I don't drink like that usually. But me and the boys got together, and one drink led to more drinks, and then to shots…."

"Lightweight," snickered Pearl.

Ben smiled and muttered, "Yeah, I guess."

Pearl placed her book down and jabbed again, "Those stacks over there aren't going to shelve themselves, shit stain. You're so lucky I don't rat you out again. I cover for you so much, and for what!"

Glancing slowly at the two carts full of haphazardly stacked books, Ben exhausted a sigh. "I know, Pearl. You've always looked out for me. I don't thank you enough." He grabbed at his burning, aching lungs and his raw esophagus. After Ben organized his thoughts, he asked, "Could I borrow your charger? My phone's completely dead."

Pearl glanced at Ben's puppy eyes and tried to mask her pity but couldn't. She smiled and opened the drawer. In it, she spotted Ida's note beside her phone charger. Her devilish wheels began to churn.

She retrieved the charger, plugged it into the wall behind her, and held her palm out for Ben's phone. He reluctantly thanked her as she plugged it in. Then Ben shuffled off toward the book carts.

By an hour into Ben's shift, Pearl had fielded three phone calls from Ida. She lied in stellar fashion, saying Ben hadn't reported to work. She also performed thorough checks of Ben's phone, deleting all of Ida's missed phone calls, frantic texts, and her voicemails. She felt he was asking for it, really—he should have used a passcode like everyone else. But he was so trusting!

She then disconnected his phone so that it teetered on one percent. Hers was a different breed of obsession.

It had occurred to her to toss Ida's note. *Heck, I've had come this far already,* she thought. She read it again, one last time:

Ben,

There's been an accident. I must go. There is a child involved. It's very complicated, and I must see to their care. I'm off to St. Bernadette Hospital in Upstate New York. Call me when you can, and I'll elaborate. I know you understand. I love you so much.

Ida

Pearl was not completely without a heart. The word 'child' had resonated with her. She knew Ida hadn't intended for Pearl to read the note. If she were ever found out, she could simply say that she had forgotten about it. She had already invaded Ben's privacy by deleting data from his phone. This was just more data.

Pearl looked up, and her wandering eye caught sight of Ben on his tippy-toes, shelving books on a top shelf. His muscular frame stretched through his body-hugging sweater and his firm bottom stood out. He had just helped an elderly man find a book. He was caring, strong, sexy, and on the precipice of being hers. She decidedly tore the note into pieces and into the trash it went.

Then, without hesitating, she grabbed her own cell phone, placed a BE BACK IN 5 sign on her desk, and slithered out of her chair. She walked with a laser-beam purpose toward Ben, then made a sharp left.

She stopped at the self-serve coffee station in the back and whipped up a piping hot cup of coffee just the way Ben liked it. Not a coffee person herself, she inhaled the distinct aroma, the one she had come to associate with Ben, as his routine at the start of every shift always began with coffee. She'd even learned to use the handheld frother to make a heart with the milk foam. With a proud devilish smile, she proceeded toward Ben.

She crept up like a gliding apparition, unexpectedly starling him.

"Shit! You scared the crap outta me!" exclaimed Ben.

Pearl steadied his cup of coffee, delicately maintaining her heart-shaped foam design. "Sorry. Didn't mean to spook you. I think I filled the cup up way too much. But I hope you like it. You sure looked like you could use it."

Ben normally received Pearl's kindness with suspicion, but this afternoon, he was operating on a significant delay.

He sipped the coffee slowly and nodded in appreciation. "It's perfect. Thanks."

Hardly one to beat around the bush, Pearl plainly said, "You know, something's not right with your girl, and I think you should know that." Ben's eyes began to roll mid-sip as Pearl continued. "Look, I've always looked out for you, haven't I? I mean, I cover when you're running late, I switch shifts with you last minute. I did score you those tickets to that off-Broadway last year and—"

Ben cut her off. "Pearl, thanks. I get it, but—"

"When I see you going down this path, one where you will only get hurt, I can't just sit and watch you get crushed. I gotta step in, ya know?"

"What path? What are you talking about?"

Pearl took a more serious tone, "Look. I've seen her with this guy, right? He's straight outta *Mad Men*. You know the type: clean cut, gel pasted hair, four-figure suit, limo, flashy Rolex, the whole nine."

Ben was exasperated. "She works in a male-dominated corporate world. They all look like that."

"Do they usually greet each other like this?" Pearl shoved Ben up onto a bookcase and then pressed herself upon him. She fondled every part of him aggressively grabbing at his chest shoulders, arms, sides and eventually his manhood. Ben tried to sidestep away but Pearl grabbed Ben by his arm with a surprisingly tight vice-grip like hold and planted a sloppy wet kiss.

Ben broke free of Pearl's clutches, spilling his coffee in the process, "Pearl!" he scolded.

Pearl's chest was heaving with adrenaline. She had kissed Ben, an achievement she had longed for since the minute Ben started working at the bookstore. She was sure she had made a convincing point, in her own distorted way. Ben deflated that hope, "Pearl, you are out of control, and out of line! That was so not cool. So not cool! I know what you're trying to do, and you better back up. I'm not in the mood today—or ever, for that matter."

Pearl was devastated. Her eyes sank in massive disappointment. But she would never easily forfeit. She fished out her phone and scrolled to her photos, then shoved the screen in Ben's face. It was a picture of Ida and the said debonair man embracing. Admittedly, the picture did not exemplify a typically professional greeting. There was more than a cordial greeting, but it wasn't the provocative, over-the-top display of public affection Pearl had claimed it was. Regardless, Ben gulped in trepidation.

"Pearl, okay, a picture says a thousand words, and not one of them is remotely close to what you're hinting at."

Pearl's wicked smile returned. "Oh, yeah? Just wait. There's more."

Chapter Twenty-one

Ida walked into the intensive care unit at St. Bernadette Hospital in Upstate New York, only thirty or so miles north of New York City but more than an hour and a half travel on a good day. She ambled with an uncharacteristically shaky gate. She had not seen Spencer for nearly three years, and it angered her that he still had a hold on her. But from all accounts, Spencer was not here. As she made her way into the waiting area, she saw Claudia, Spencer's daughter from an earlier relationship.

Claudia was now sixteen years old, and a sophomore in high school. The moment her and Ida's eyes met, tears swelled, and memories exploded like a bursting dam. They quickly hurried to each other and embraced. To see this girl budding into a young woman was breathtaking on many levels, and just as heartbreaking.

When Ida entered into her world, Claudia was just a toddler. Ida had never wanted to see Spencer again, but she'd missed this young girl every day since she left. Over time, she'd grown to love Claudia as her own, even though Spencer had shared custody of her, and they only saw her a few weekends a month. That in and of itself was a joke, as Spencer had often neglected Claudia or, worse, pawned her off on Ida entirely. Ida chastised herself for not realizing just how selfish and detached Spencer had been to his own child.

He was never physically abusive, and probably knew that if he had been, Ida would have knocked him into tomorrow. But what Spencer was, was a master manipulator. He held a PhD in guilt. You all know the type. Twisting words against you, rephrasing responses to make you feel dumb, and trying to get you to see ambiguity where it really does not exist. He once argued with Ida ad nauseam that the earth may, indeed, be flat—and for a second she considered it. Ida had noticed Spencer pulling the same nonsense on young Claudia, and she would step in often. As a result, Spencer duped Ida into taking her to dance practices, playdates, recitals, trips to the park, and even, once, a parent–teacher conference. As a result, Ida had ended up caring a lot about Claudia.

The parallels to Ida's own upbringing struck a chord buried deep within her. She knew that an important comfort when growing up in a split home was a mainstay of kindness and a safe haven somewhere or in someone. For her, it had been her grandmother. For Claudia, it was Ida, who so desperately wanted to compensate for the shortcomings of her own childhood through her relationship with Claudia. In doing so, she'd overextended her patience for Spencer's bullshit. Ida enjoyed Claudia's company, but it was an awkward position to be in. She grew more and more conflicted as she grew apart from Spencer. But there was a cap to just how much Ida could take.

In the end, she cut the line to save herself, but Claudia and others had been at the other end. Spencer, in his infinite self-centeredness, never stopped letting her know that.

It weighed heavy on her heart, like a two-thousand-pound albatross. She had suppressed her relationship with Claudia deep within her subconscious, to the point that it had become the one thing she just could not articulate to Ben, and at times and not even to herself. But she realized it now, with Claudia in her arms.

When Ben revealed how his ex had an abortion without discussing it with him, she could tell it had devastated him. She sensed how delicate that topic was, so she chose to not mention Claudia. So, when Kurt had brought up Brielle, the dog she'd lost in the breakup, she knew what he was hinting at. He'd wanted Ida to come clean with everything, and not trip over the skeleton bones in the closet. She'd hated him for it at time, and even now she could picture Kurt gloating, "I told you so!"

As they disentangled and wiped their tears, Ida blubbered, "Oh, my goodness, look at you! You're right as rain! Wait so you weren't hurt?"

"No, not really. I was in the back seat and buckled in. This guy ran the light and hit our car head-on. The paramedics called it a 'T-bone' I think."

"Oh, my."

"Yeah. I was knocked around a bit, and my side is sore. My mom got hit bad. They put her in a medically induced coma. She's stable, but she's gonna be laid up awhile."

"I'm so sorry. The message I received said you were involved. I feared the worst but look at you! I must say what a gorgeous peach you are!"

Claudia stood nearly eye level with Ida, who was slightly taller than average. What's more, Ida was standing in her high heels. Claudia could only muster a childish blush and a bashful smile.

Ida made sure to remain cheerful and tender. "How are you holding up?"

Claudia responded in a sheepish tone, "Fine."

Ida shook her head in doubtful acceptance, then shot straight from the hip as always: "So, your mother is in a medially induced coma, your father is your father, wherever he's holed up, you are in your second year of high school, and you're *fine*? Honestly, do I have to hit the BS button?"

Claudia's composure collapsed, and she nodded with watery eyes. But in cold hearted fashion, she sucked up her tears and callously dismissed, "Well, it's not like this any difference than before."

Ida was shocked at how icy Claudia had responded and eerily reminded her of Spencer. "Claudia, she's far from 'Mom of the Year', but she's still your mother!"

Claudia looked away and shrugged her shoulders in that defiant teenage show of strength commonly mistaken for indifference and sighed, "Whatever."

Ida had to draw back and re-focus. She refrained from an all-out tongue lashing and tried her hardest to switch angles and perspective. The short period of time that Ida had been way, much has happened. The teenage years are rough and even made more taxing on a young woman neglected by her mother and estranged by her father. Spencer did not have to cast his guilt net here. Ida was entangled deep in it all by herself.

Ida drew her in for a consoling squeeze but Claudia now took a flaccid and lifeless posture. Futilely, Ida said, "Life is anything but easy, my dear. There are rough patches on roads we did not choose to walk down, but that's the way it goes."

Claudia raised her eyebrows and rolled her eyes in a pathetic non-verbal sign of 'sure'.

Ida had brokered dealings with some of the most rude, crude and bigoted old boys of the establishment always finding a diplomatic way to seal the deal. Here with a sixteen-year-old young lady, she was utterly lost as too how to approach her.

From the corner of her eyes, Ida noticed a food cart and had thought, "Care for some tea?"

Claudia smiled half-heartedly, shrugged her shoulders again and made a semblance of a nod. Ida took Claudia by the arm and strolled out of the waiting area and toward the cafeteria. As they walked, Claudia leaned onto Ida like a crutch as they proceeded in silence.

In the cafeteria, Ida directed Claudia to take a seat in a far corner of the expansive dining area. Meanwhile, she prepared two cups of tea, then brought them over. The echo of her high heels sounded as out of place as Ida looked in her power suit in the backdrop if scrubs, lab coats and the casual attire of visitors. The lunchroom was a sparkling, bright white, sterile and unfeeling. The exact sort of place you wouldn't want to have an estranged relationship reunion, especially under as dire a circumstance as a car crash.

Claudia gratefully accepted the tea and blew gently to cool the steeping beverage. She seemed foggy and aloof, lost in thought as she stared at the steam rising from the cup. After taking the first sip, she smiled and looked up at Ida with big, fond eyes. "No one makes tea quite like you, Ida."

Ida fought hard to not burst into tears and moved quickly to respond, "So, I fancy there are a lot of naughty boys at your school? A motley bunch of unruly chaps, I imagine?"

Claudia bashfully looked up at just about every corner of the ceiling tiles, unsuccessfully fighting off a guilty grin.

"Come on, a bright blossom such as yourself most definitely would attract pests of all sorts. It's okay. It's natural, darling. Just make sure those vultures treat you like a proper lady, respectful and courteous, and then you may turn them down gently, or otherwise as appropriate. You're all in this together. It's just Their hormones want to smash, and yours want to dance. So, nothing serious, for now. Have a ball with it."

"Yes ma'am," huffed Claudia causing Ida to inhale deeply, testing her tolerance.

Ida quipped, "I hopelessly try to forget those lonely and awkward years, all the missteps have helped me be where I am today."

A brief pause filled the air, with Ida uneasily waiting a response and Claudia holding court in which direction this conversation will head.

Finally, Claudia spoke in a cautious approach, "Awkward? I mean I thought you were and am the most beautiful and strong woman I've ever known. How could it have been awkward for you?"

Ida smiled, "My dear, understand this, these years are awkward for everyone. Everyone thinks they know where they want to go and who they want to be but knows one knows how and so it's like learning to walk all over again." She drew in a tense breath before finishing, "Your father and I had our moments, good and bad, and because I had some unresolved issues, I stayed longer than I should have. But I don't outright regret those years and watching you grow up and some of those memories I will fondly take to my grave. But as you will learn, life is about falling down, getting up, walking, falling down, getting up, repeat. Just don't trip over the same bump in the road twice. Then shame on you."

Claudia continued to be a challenge to read. Her face seemed expressionless. Then is deadpan matter of fact tone she uttered, "I wish my dad wasn't such a fucking asshole and my mom wasn't such a fucking loser too. They don't give two shits about me. I'm just a thing they have to take care of because the courts say so."

Claudia didn't even trickle a tear. It was painfully obvious to Ida that Claudia had resolved this for some time now. To hear it just be directly affirmed and with spitfire cursing rendered speechless. She placed her hand over Claudia's listless and unresponsive hand. Ever since she had known Claudia's mom, she was a train wreck, with an on and off relationship with booze, drugs and men. The men all had the same personality, abusive, manipulative and transient. In many ways they were all Spencer recycled. Ida felt like she was not one to preach having endured Spencer for so long. But Ida was different. She drew the lines hard and fast. But she always fell short of a full cut off. The strong willed and confident Ida had an emotional void; it was her one soft spot. Desperately she didn't want it to be Claudia's.

Suddenly, Claudia withdrew her hand slowly. Ida was taken a back and made a wonderous face but did not speak.

Claudia continued in her plain tone, "I'm sixteen now and I think I can be on my own now and…"

Claudia paused as if she had revealed too much. Ida slowly responded, "You very well can. But like I said, we all fall but it helps when there are people around to help you back up. You can always lean on me if you need a place to crash or advise or even a few bucks…"

The teen angst returned as Claudia shook her head in disbelief, "Yeah, sure."

Ida positioned her face in Claudia's field of view and affirmed, "I'm here aren't I? I have no obligation to except that I want to be here for you. That's all I can say about that misstatement."

Claudia leaned back and lamented, "Things all went to shit once you left…" And then the floodgates opened as she burst into tears. Ida engulfed her and understood every word."

Chapter Twenty-two

Pearl showed Ben picture after picture of Ida with this mysterious, dapper man. She had even cropped close-up shots. Ben was slow to respond, as the shock was overwhelming. He had asked several times to go back and forth between the photos before impatient Pearl just gave him her phone. He studied them for hidden signals that would end his growing suspicions.

After five minutes, Ben asked, "Let me get this straight. You've been spying on Ida?"

"What!" an incensed Pearl exclaimed. "No, you ingrateful assclown! I thought you'd want to know when your being dicked in the ass. You're fucking welcome!"

Pearl rolled her eyes as Ben digested the photos and their meaning. He was trying his best to be reasonable and consider Ida innocent until proven guilty. He reminded himself that the shoe could easily have been on the other foot; photos of Pearl wrapping him in one of her many over-the-top hugs. Those could very easily be misconstrued, even if the thought did make him shudder. He was trying desperately to hold it together, especially in front of Pearl. Inside was a different story. The ugly head of his anxiety kept peeking into his fragile psyche.

Ben then demanded, "Can I have my phone now?"

Pearl nonchalantly walked over to her desk, retrieved his phone, and walked deathly slow back to Ben and handed it to him. Ben turned it on to find a display of 1% charge. "Son of a—"

Pearl quipped, "Maybe when you dropped it in the bar last night and it messed something up inside." She finished with a half-assed smile to equal her half-assed excuse for little to no charge.

Ben quietly said, "I'm going to take a hard five right now."

Pearl tried to be helpful. "Want a toke to ease you a bit?" She dangled her weed pen.

Ben politely declined, then proceeded to walk around a stationary Pearl and exit the bookstore. Outside, Ben drew in a deep, cleansing breath and ruffled his unkept bird's nest of a hairdo. The crisp, cool air filled his lungs and downshifted his revving mind. Before an all-out panic attack took hold, Ben needed to close his eyes and clear his head. Usually, it took ten minutes or so, to get away from everything. He would slow his breathing and repeat to himself some of the mantras Dr. Hoda had taught him. He walked around the corner, out of Pearl's sight, and paused in the shadow of a huge marble skyscraper. The stone slab wall was cold, and there Ben raised his palms to his eyelids and slowed his inhalations, repeating to himself the mantras.

First: *I'm okay. I'm slowing myself down the hill until coming to a complete stop.*

Second: *I am in control of what I can control.*

Third: *What is the objective? Concentrate on the objective.*

Ben had to repeat these slower and slower each time until each phrase lasted a full minute. By then his breathing was so slow and even he might as well have been napping. He had learned to be grounded and calm before anything else. Then, and only then, could he act, and not just react or overreact.

Except today, he was struggling.

Once he'd calmed himself, Ben walked the three-and-a-half blocks to Ida's office. He stopped to contemplate the surroundings. This looked a lot like where Ida and that mysterious fellow had been locked in an ambiguous embrace. The panic of having the rug pulled out from under him started to tighten his chest again. Even in public on this frigid day, Ben felt his grip on composure quickly loosening. Gathering his focus on the objective, he concentrated on his phone. Ben pivoted and darted into a nearby electronics store. There, Ben paced up and down the aisle mechanically, scanning everything and registering nothing. Internally, he was reciting the calming mantras in double time, looking very disturbed, until a salesman approached him and said, "How can I help you, sir?"

Startled, Ben stood motionless and speechless.

But the salesman persisted. "Are you looking for anything in particular? Cell phone perhaps? Camera? Souvenir? We have new Statue of Liberties and Empire State Buildings. They light up, LED. Fun, fun, fun! I show you."

Ben finally snapped out of his doldrums. "Ah, yeah, do you have a charger for this phone?" He held up his phone, for the first time noticing the cracked screen and scuff marks, feeling a bizarre connection to its fractured physical state and to his internal one. His cloud nine ride had suddenly been free-falling back to earth and he was in need of some sort of parachute before crashing into a plume of unrecognizable parts.

"Right here, my friend."

"Okay, great. How much?"

"Usually twenty-nine ninety-nine, my friend, but for you, today, special, twenty dollars with purchase of Statue of Liberty or Empire

State Building. Come on, friend, give to special lady."

"Not really interested." Ben was painfully sensitive to the "special lady" comment, and apparently had been very transparent about it.

"Lady give you headache?"

"Headache? No, heartache is more like it. I got a bit of a head-scratcher today."

He was not sure if the salesman understood his murmur. The salesman kept chiseling. "We have Tylenol, Advil, Excedrin my friend."

Ben processed, "Ah, Tylenol, I suppose."

As the salesman rang him up, he took an interest in Ben's dejected mug and tossed in a stuffed heart that bore the famous NY logo with his charger and medication. "On the house, my friend."

Ben simply shrugged his shoulders and expressed a half-hearted thanks.

As he left the store, Ben took a few sad steps before noticing the black limo cruise past him and toward Ida's building. His heart stopped, dropped, and burst like a blown tire. He watched the vehicle until it came to a stop right in front of her office building.

Chapter Twenty-three

The rear passenger door opened and the blond man from the pictures emerged stopping Ben's heart. His hair was gelled back, dark, and tight, but his top was a straw-colored blond. He wore a dark blue pinstripe suit under his thick black overcoat. He was tall and well-framed. His face was lean and square, with a charming smile. He was elegant and streamlined, eye-catchingly handsome.

The man walked around the limo, opened the other door, and held out his hand like a gentleman. Ida's unmistakable hand took hold of his as he helped her out of the car. Ben's heart stopped again. He watched them both exchange some cheerful words, accompanied by laughter, and then a very long and smothering hug.

For Ben, it was a two by four strike to his forehead.

In their embrace, Ida whispered to Eddie, Spencer's brother, "I am so sorry, and I hope for the best for Claudia. I'd love to help out when I can, but I am in a different place now and starting something new. I hope you can understand that. Let's touch base, see how Claudia holds up. I know this is difficult, but I also don't want to…"

"Say no more," Eddie said, his voice steady and even as he placed his finger onto Ida's lips. "Again, everything is touch and go right now. Claudia will stay with us, and we appreciate the offer you put out to her. You don't have to."

Ida peered back into the vehicle and remined, "My door is always open to you my dear."

Eddie's little girl, Geneva, dressed in a white faux fur coat adorably asked, "For me too?"

"Absolutely my dear."

"We always consider you family, Ida."

They embraced again as Ben watched from afar. It felt like a dagger digging deeper into its mark.

 She kissed the man on the cheek—or was it the lips? Ben's imagination couldn't tell.

She waved into the car, perplexing Ben even more. Then, as she stepped away, a young girl in a white fur coat came storming after her. Their embrace was even more emotional than Ida's had been with the mystery man.

Ben watched in confused horror, not knowing what to make of all this. His soul was being torn to shreds. His pulse raced, nearly collapsing him.

Geneva jumped out of the car door and gave Ida one last tight hug. The dagger now emerged right through Ben's heart penetrating through and through. Not privy to dialogue nor to the backdrop, ben was only limited to what his eyes witnessed and all of Pearl's deep cutting words seem to ring true.

Was Pearl right all along? Was Ida keeping a secret life from him? Did he not figure into her life like the suits did?

Ben nearly fainted at the sight grasping onto the wall of the building to stop him from collapsing right then and there. It was torture of the highest order, unbearable for both his mind and his soul.

He took in a deep breath and tried to shake himself back to reality. He had had enough thought. Resolved and determined, Ben began to march up to her and demand answers when Meck's SUV pulled up suddenly. His burning tires and the acrid smell of brake pads stopped Ben in his tracks.

Meck lowered his window and yelled, "Yo, where you been, bro? The world has been looking for you! I thought you got your phone back?"

Ben was hit from angle today and struggled to answer. "I…I was just at the bookstore. I got my phone back from the bar before that. It's dead though; it won't charge. I had to buy a stupid charger. Why, what's up?"

Meck shook his head. "Get in."

"I can't. I gotta settle some major shit with Ida. I don't know what the hell is—"

Meck interrupted, "That can wait." Meck dramatically paused staring off into the distance. He usually deals directly and in your face. Something was definitely wrong. When his eyes returned to Ben, they were sad. "We gotta head back to your place."

"My place? Why?"

Meck remained silent and sullen. It took a moment for Ben register and then uttered in horrified realization, "Buddy."

Chapter Twenty-four

By the time Meck and Ben pulled up to his apartment building, Ben's anxiety had hit an all-time high. His legs were visibly shaking, and his hands fidgeted and pulled at his curly hair. Meck tried his best to calm him, but quickly realized all his efforts would be in vain. Once Ben saw the ambulance, his last shred of composure dropped to the pit of his gut and ripped right through it. Next to the ambulance was a dark blue dented van with a side decal that read New York City Medical Examiner. The sight of that van made him gag, but there was nothing in his stomach.

Without waiting for Meck to come to a full stop, Ben opened the door and rolled out. He didn't quite stick the landing, but managed to scramble toward the ambulance. Its lights were twirling, but it was empty. He then turned his head slowly toward the blue medical examiner van. His tentative inspection noticed that this van was empty too. Ben set his eyes on the apartment building, pacing slowly now toward the main lobby doors. A numb sensation radiated throughout his body, pulsating with greater vibrations every few steps. It was like he could watch himself in a surreal slow-motion reel, complete with the staticky background hiss of old film and a grainy visual to match.

From the minute he woke up, he'd felt he had lost all grip on reality, levied by bombshell after heart-stomping bombshell.

In the lobby was an officer speaking coded jargon into a hand-held radio. The cop avoided any kind of eye contact and carried on as if Ben wasn't even there. He was staring at everyone and everything, trying to piece together clues about what exactly was happening, denying with every step what his gut and eyes knew to be true.

As he ascended up the stairs, a few more scattered EMS personnel and one other officer meandered about, treating Ben as if he were the invisible man himself. Ben stopped about three feet from his apartment door. It was wide open, and the ramblings of disjointed radio chatter emanated from within. The cold reality of probability was creeping in fast.

He wasn't even sure he was breathing at this point. Every sound was echoing, as though coming from a distance, and not intended for his ears. He wanted to wake up from this bad, bad daydream, but his legs kept moving him forward. He continued in a slow procession, with thoughts of a quick retreat. At the doorway, he could no longer feel or hear his own heartbeat, but he swore he could have heard even the smallest insect breathing. He reminded himself to exhale.

A man wearing a weathered, dirty, reflector-covered jacket greeted him at the doorway. "Benito Williams?"

Ben nodded; that was the best he could muster.

I'm Officer Whalen Jensen of the Office of the Chief Medical Examiner. There has been an unfortunate occurrence here. I regretfully inform you that Mr. Norbert Wilder has passed away. I'm so sorry. We can't assess when exactly and we can only speculate it may have been a cardiac event, but it's likely more than twenty-four hours. Neighbors called in with concerns. Again, I'm sorry.

Ben mouthed, "More than twenty-four hours..."

Officer Whalen had a few procedural matters to discuss with Ben, such as burial options, belongings, and a death certificate. In the officer's hands was a fistful of papers for Ben to sign, and a few papers for him to keep. But it was all a blur, one bad nightmare that seemed to unfold slower with every passing second. He couldn't take his attention away from the hallway. There, some people from other technicians and a pair of paramedics were shooting the breeze next to a slick black body bag.

Ben raced toward it and unzipped it before anyone could stop him. Officer Whalen, all three hundred pounds of him, trailed behind in lumbering pursuit.

But then he gave up. Officer Whalen held his hands up and waved off any interference. In an instant, the crew knew exactly what was happening. They mumbled to each other about getting some coffee. They had worked this gig long enough to know when to give a little space. They all exited, except for Officer Whalen, who lingered in the background.

Ben began to whimper and berate himself. "I should have been here for you. It was my job to help out. I..." The words were soon drowned out by a full-blown cry full of deep remorse as Ben dropped to his knees beside Buddy.

Officer Whalen rounded the corner to give Ben some privacy. He too had a routine in situations such as this. In about ten minutes, he would ease Ben off Buddy's lifeless body and recite rehearsed lines of comfort. At some point, he had to could transport Buddy's body to the main city morgue for storage, and to await burial proceedings. In cases of financial hardship or unclaimed deceased, the city would provide a burial at the county plot.

Eventually, the officer would relay to Ben that Buddy was found slumped over in the bathroom—a common site, actually, where strain under already stressful circumstances can exacerbate other conditions, leading to death.

It had not occurred to Ben how he would finance Buddy's funeral and burial and if he had any funds from the military or even a will with preset arrangements. Truthfully, Ben had been too consumed with guilt to clearly think things through. As soon as Buddy had been transported out of the apartment, Ben plopped himself down onto the ragged couch and lamented. He remained silent and still and stared into nothingness, wrought with emotions that tore at him like a particles in the Large Hadron Collier, flying at ridiculous speeds, and with extreme force, smashing to bits thousands of times over and over.

In the last twenty-four hours, Ben had lost his phone, seen suspicious evidence of a possible secret intimate relationship Ida was having, witnessed with his own eyes that supposed secret relationship, discovered the death of his roommate and now his mental stability hung in limbo. It had been a slow-roasting dumpster fire of a day, and Ben was beside himself.

The demons of his depression and anxiety were knocking and knocking hard. It was coming full force, and they were on the verge of breaking down the door.

Chapter Twenty-five

About an hour has passed since Ben dropped his listless self on the couch. Ben sat motionless since. He sank into the cushions, alternating between tears and lamentations; he was a blank portrait of despair. Then his phone rang. Meck had given the phone a little juice on the car ride over.

Ben was unresponsive and unmoved. He didn't even bother to check who was calling. He let the call go to voicemail. But not a minute later, the phone rang again. This time, after the fourth ring, he glanced at the caller ID. It was Ida calling. He hesitated before covering it with a pillow and letting it go to voicemail again. His mailbox was full, but he did not seem to care, especially for her.

The pictures of her and that guy were still painfully fresh in his mind, just like the image of Buddy's dead body on a gurney. Pearl's sinister seeds of doubt and his own stunned eyes had painted a dark mosaic of red and purple squirls of anger; hurt and guilt boiled his blood. Then there was that little girl. Who was she? All the layers of images sent Ben spiraling down the toilet bowl of depression.

During the car ride, Meck had added gasoline to this already roaring blaze by lecturing Ben, "Don't be tricked by the booty! You are spending way too much time with her. You forgetting about yourself! Bitches are a dime a dozen. If they become a problem, pass them up, move em up and move on out."

These 'problems' than he could handle were beginning to mount. His self-loathing was hitting an all-time high. His eyes landed on his medication of generic Xanax on top of the counter. The paramedics must have foraged through all his meds, prescriptions and over-the-counters, everything and anything to rule out any potentially fatal interactions or overdoses, accidental or intentional. It seemed like all the medications in the house were lined up on the counter, but only one bottle stood out to Ben.

He stared at the bottle for an eternity. Ben slowly stood up and trudged toward the counter. He reached for the bottle and read it thoroughly, re-reading the dosage, side effects, and warnings. Then he held it in a tight grip as he trembled and teared, wrestling with what to do next. He looked around the living room in search of any inspiration, hoping a sign would help him decide on what to do next. He pleaded for the spirts of Buddy, his father, his mother, and deity any one and anything. There was no such sign – only silence.

He rubbed his chest and throat, still strained from all the heavy breathing, and this morning's vomiting episode. His physical body was achy and numb and wasted. His mind was incoherent. His emotions lay fragmented in an endless wasteland.

He then glanced back at the congregation of pill bottles that had belonged to Buddy. It sobered him to realize just how much medication his roommate was taking, how much pain he had hidden from him and perhaps how much Ben failed to want to see. Buddy's health had been deteriorating, and eventually he died alone. That's the wound that hurt the most.

Ben slowly placed the bottle back on the counter. He scanned the room with sore eyes and realized he could not stay here.

Then his phone buzzed in succession, over and over again. When he checked it, message notifications were bombarding his screen. Ben grew irate.

Chapter Twenty-six

Ida stared blankly at her computer screen. Uncharacteristically, she could not concentrate on her work. Her mind shifted constantly, wondering why Ben had not contacted her. She stopped calling the bookstore after the fifth futile time. Pearl had been quickly dismissing of her concerns and excusing herself, saying she was "super busy." The clock on Ida's monitor read 4:45 p.m. She knew the bookstore would be closing early today. It was New Year's Eve after all.

Ida checked her phone for the billionth time. Still no missed calls, no text messages, no voicemail, no nothing. She had had enough. *To hell with Pearl.*

Ida grabbed her phone, her keys, and her purse, threw on her coat, and rushed out of her office. She zoomed past Carmen, wished her a rushed "Happy New Year," and squeezed into the jam-packed elevator. She was at the Abbey May Bookstore in a record-breaking five minutes, trotting in at lightning speed despite her high heels and having to navigate the crowded sidewalks filled with would-be participants of the Times Square New Year's Eve countdown celebration.

Pearl was ten feet away from flipping the CLOSED sign when Ida burst through the doors. Pearl stopped dead in her tracks, wearing a pale face of guilt and fear. Ida's chest rose and fell with a frightful determined look. Her hair was splayed in all directions and seemed as electrically charged as she was. But her face was dead serious, and in no mood for any bullshit.

She spat out, "Where's Ben?"

Pearl causally replied, "Who?"

Ida tilted her head slightly, holding down the venom boiling inside of her.

Before Ida could utter a word of contempt, Pearl stuttered, "I mean, Ben, of course. He came in late and in a real hurry. He looked pissed off, so I let him be. Then just like that, he left in hurry. The boss ain't gonna be happy."

"Screw the boss. Did you give him the note or not?"

Pearl was a world class liar and confronted by an irate Ida, she hesitated, and her eyes betrayed her, as they constantly looked away. She eventually cracked, "Ah, yeah. Of course. I think that's when he stormed off." She capped it with a hint of a smugness.

Ida returned with a smug look of her own as she slowly stepped toward Pearl, who backed up in growing apprehension. "We're closed now. But we're open all day on the second."

Ida spoke in slowly paced words, over-pronouncing each syllable for effect. "Perjury is defined as lying under oath in court, punishable up to five years in prison. Lying to me will be far, far worse. Might I remind you: I have dual citizenship. I could go to England, should I be extradited for any one of heinous, albeit righteous crimes."

Ida closed in on Pearl and stopped only inches away from Pearl's face with a death-wish like seriousness about her.

Pearl was having second thoughts. "Oh, you know, in all the hustle and bustle of the day, I must have forgotten. He was in such a rush."

Ida's eyes remained locked onto Pearl's. The tense stretch of silence only heard the heavy breaths of Ida and the quick breaths of Pearl.

Finally, Ida took a few measured steps backward and tossed her hair in defiance, all the while maintaining her dead-red stare at Pearl. "I just can't place it. Not yet. But when I get down to the nitty gritty of it all, I'm sure you are at the rotten core of this and this will not end well for you. Mark my words." With that, Ida spun a flawless one-eighty degree turn, then stomped out of the bookstore. Her heels struck an extra sharp tap with each step.

Once Ida was out of sight, Pearl tentatively walked up to the door, locked it, then turned the sign around. From the window she watched Ida hail a cab, get in, and speed off. Pearl grinned. "Oh yeah? Well, it ain't gonna end well for *you*, bitch."

Pearl grabbed her phone and scrolled through with a cresting, plotting smirk.

Chapter Twenty-seven

Ben huffed and puffed, pacing feverishly in the living room, arguing with himself in a mix of mumbles, curses, and hair pulls. He pounded on the wall with frustration, cutting and bruising his fists slightly spraining his right wrist. Pearl had sent him all the photos she had, along with some choice words. His head was spinning off its post. He felt the presence of Buddy all around him, weighing on him as well. Every photo he saw seemed to blare with a background audio of jeers and mocking laughs. Anger was displacing his guilt, and that further infuriated Ben. He was just about ready to explode.

His phone rang again as he scrolled through the photos again. It was Ida. After four rings, he finally picked up, and she snapped at him, "Well, hello from the dead! Where the hell have you been?"

Ben vehemently lashed out. "That's not at all funny! So absolutely not funny right now!"

"Pardon? You've been MIA for the better part of the day and it's been one heck of a day, might I add. You have no idea what I've been going through!"

Ben was still stuck at her initial greeting. "It was not a funny joke."

"What? What is the matter with you!"

"Life is a fucking joke! *This* is a joke. It's all lies and bullshit!"

"Ben, what is the matter? What is lies and bullshit? I've had a very trying day, and I desperately wanted to speak with you. I have been trying to reach you all damn day—"

"Trying day? Trying day! I'll tell you what's a trying fucking day!" Ben was silent for a few seconds before declaring in resonating pain, "Buddy is dead. He is *dead*, Ida. And you know what? He fucking died alone. All alone! I was not here. I haven't been here, and I should have! Maybe If I were here he's would still be alive. And to top it all off, you're all over town smooching some slick Don Juan, toasting it up rich and famous style!"

Silence filled the air. Ida was completely dumbfounded. She finally broke down. "Oh, Dear Ben, I'm so sorry. I'm sorry about Buddy...but I don't have a clue what else you're alluding to!"

Ben remained quiet.

Ida proceeded with caution. "I had no idea. How..."

"Doesn't matter. He's gone. If I had been here...if I had just been here, maybe I could've called for an ambulance or something."

"Oh, Ben. Are you there now? I'll come right over."

"Why don't you just stay with that pretty blond suit?" lashed Ben.

"What is all this? What are you talking about?"

"Pearl filled me in on your little meetings with that Mister fancy pants, limo-riding man-about-town."

"Pearl? Man-about-town?"

"She showed me pictures Ida! I have picture after picture of you and that other guy you've been seeing. Apparently, we haven't had that exclusive relationship you wanted so much!"

"Guy I'm seeing? I'm seeing you and only you, Ben. And I getting deeply offended here."

Ben ratcheted up his tone. "Come on already. I have all these pics, and God knows what else there is that I haven't seen."

"Stop right there, before you say anything else!"

"Enough with the bullshit already! I saw it with my own two eyes. My phone died, and when I went out to buy a charger, I saw you come out of the same limo Pearl had seen you come out of a dozen times and hug that very same dude, and then some little kid! I saw it, Ida, with my own two fucking eyes! So, what, do you have a secret family I should know about? I mean what the fuck!"

"Oh, my goodness, Ben! What you saw was a friend and his daughter! How could you doubt me? I am telling you the truth! This is some dreadful mis…"

"You know what? Save it. Who fucking cares? All bullshit walks, Ida! The world is bullshit, I'm bullshit! You're bullshit! Just…who freaking cares anyway? I don't. I don't care anymore. Life is fucking pointless! It's all shit!"

With that, Ben hung up his phone, turned it off, and tossed it onto the couch. The dam had broken. He could feel radiating, pulsating anger course through his veins as he breathed deeply. The air was thinly filling. He became claustrophobic in his own skin. He felt tightness everywhere. If he could, he would have ripped through his own skin, dived into frigid cold artic waters, and sank submissively into the dark abyss.

He took hold of the bottle of the Benzodiazepine, Xanax and struggled with, growing more contemptuous with rotation. Finally, he twisted it open violently, spilling pills all over the counter and the kitchen floor. He picked up a couple and shoved them into his mouth, swallowing it dry. He nearly choked on the dryness of the pills and its unnatural sensation. Ben wedged his head under the sink and gulped tap water straight from New York's finest reservoirs—through corroded and possibly lead-lined pipes.

Then he grabbed his keys, his phone, and a beer from the fridge and stormed out of the apartment.

Chapter Twenty-eight

In her bedroom, Ida sat motionless, staring at herself in the vanity. She was dressed in a full-body sexy lace outfit and a black mini skirt, with a white silk scarf draped over her breasts and nothing more. This was supposed to have been a magical night, a sensual and spectacular ushering in of the new year. She had been planning this evening for weeks, and it had all crumbled in a less-than-two-minute phone call.

Ida was distraught. She suddenly feeling foolish and silly wearing her outfit when the torched nerve of accusation was still raw and throbbing.

Ida had not even occurred to Ida that Ben was talking about Eddie. Eddie, as he was part of her past relationship. Unfortunately, he was now a part of her present. When Ben had mentioned the limo today, the lightning quick speed of todays' events came to an abrupt and sudden stop. It was indeed Eddie he was talking about. Ben's words scorched her, but she was still piecing the puzzle together now with sobering clarity. She realized, above all, that in light of Buddy's death, Ida could give more leeway than she normally would. It was also Ben speaking to her with such hurtful words. It dug in deeper, but it also meant he was speaking from a bad, bad place.

She looked into the mirror and scoffed at any possible romantic involvement between her and Eddie, considering she had known him for thirteen years. In any long-term relationship you get attached to friends and family, which become unfortunate casualties of the breakup. But her thoughts were a gateway down memory lane, and she had surprisingly more good memories than bad. But when she recalled the stand-out bad memories especially towards the end of the relationship, there was nothing to regret. She had to end things.‑

Then her thoughts drifted to Pearl. Her eyebrow crinkled, and she squinted into her recollection of today's whirlwind sequence of events.

Pearl had lied about the note, then only confessed when threatened. She had apparently taken pictures Ida and Eddie together, but they didn't meet more than two or three times, so Pearl must have been a Photoshop whiz, doctoring multiple condemning shots. Seen in a skewed and staged angle, the images were incriminating. Even still, how could Ben damn her, and so quickly!

Ida reprimanded herself. Buddy had just died. Ben must have discovered him and been devastated. Naturally, he had blamed himself. Pearl had struck at the right time, and the seeds of doubt she planted were flourishing in Ben's grief and vulnerable state.

Ida sat hoping that Ben's overreaction was fueled by Buddy's death. She knew that even though she'd never been so open and honest with anybody before, there was still much more she could do for Ben. She felt that if there was still a shred of trust within Ben, they could sort this out. This was not some lover or some boyfriend tiff. This was Ben, her sudden everything.

She had a moment of clarity: Ben, and their relationship, was worth every shred of energy it would take to fight for and to keep. An inner voice reminded her of how he made her feel: free and loved, the way no man ever could make her feel. She needed to go to him, and now.

But first, she had to get out of this lace.

Chapter Twenty-nine

Ben was a shattered mess. He meandered aimlessly through the city streets like a strung-out crackhead. The ill-advised consumption of Xanax and beer was beginning to affect Ben. His gait was more of a wobble, unbalanced, with irregular strides and with a bias lean to the left for some reason. His reality was bending and twisting and his sense of time was incalculable.

It was getting bitterly cold, and he was severely underdressed. All that sheltered him from the biting winds of winter were a black hooded sweatshirt under a faded gray denim jacket. His jeans had rips at the thighs and knees, allowing the piercing frosty air easy access. Although his thick hair provided some insulation, the wind chill factor howled right through it, laughing into his reddening, numbed ears. The 'Real Feel' temperature was in the teens and dropping to single digits. No gloves or mittens meant that his frozen fingers had to seek shelter in his thinly lined pants pockets. His cheeks glossed with the pink hue of frost bite.

He stumbled like a walking zombie, obliviously walking into parking meters, hydrants, lampposts, and the occasional group of festive partygoers. Crowds split around him, as he obnoxiously obstructed anyone's straight-line right-of-way. On a night like this, no one was in a mood for a game with a human pinball.

Eventually, a large group of mostly guys and a few gals approached. They were more raucous than others—clearly the party had started hours ago for them. The unmistakable scent of marijuana mixed with a whiff of hops hovered over them like the dust cloud around Pig-Pen from the famed *Peanuts* cartoon strip.

Ben had bumped square into the one of them, named Omar, causing Omar to lose his balance and trip into the street. As luck would have it, Omar was the alpha male of the pack with a penchant for brawling.

"Yo! What the hell, motherfucker!" cursed Omar.

Ben tried to verbalize but was so withdrawn and slurry that he could only blink furiously with his mouth agape.

"What's wrong with you, dumb-dumb!" another shouted.

"Watch where you're fucking walking, asshole!" one women blared.

"He's stupid or something! Fuckin retard!" piled on another.

Another guy in the group, Colin, shoved Ben in the back, causing Ben to stumble forward, smashing into the others. They took turns bouncing Ben into the middle of their circle like a mosh pit. Ben was already swirly, but now he was spinning like a dreidel about to collapse on to its side.

Omar came from nowhere to do just that. He landed a stiff right cross into Ben's left cheek, flattening him out onto a heap of trash bags by the curb. "Serves you right, you piece of shit!"

Omar topped off his profanity-laden tirade by spitting on Ben. "Stupid ass jerk!"

They all laughed and jeered in an indecipherable barrage of curses as they took turns kicking him and spitting at him while he was down. Ben curled into an instinctive defensive fetal position. The only benefit to his drug-induced sleepwalk was that the haymakers hadn't stung all that much. But tomorrow would be a different, painful story. Ben may very well not even know what had happened. As kind a soul as Ben was, he would never back down from a fight. He was always first to defend the outcasts in school, picked on because of every superficial immature reason. He was first to take a punch for a friend and last to leave the vulnerable ones to their own devices. But ironically, he couldn't lift a finger to save himself. And now, depressed and despondent, he had no fight left in him.

Out of nowhere a police siren sounded, and the thugs scattered like crows. As Ben lay there, lip cut open, side throbbing, and heart broken, a doorman named Lenox quickly approached. He had watching the trail end of the beatdown from his post, behind the glass doors of The Royal Penguin Towers residential apartment building. As Ben looked up, the streetlights above gave Lenox a halo glow. *Am I dead?* he thought.

"Easy there. They gone now! You okay?" asked Lenox in a thick West Indian accent.

Ben faintly heard the words but did not respond.

Lenox shook him again. "Hey, can you hear me, boy?"

Ben raised his arms to his face in protective defense reflex, futilely protecting what was left of himself. He then opened one eye cautiously, taking a few moments to register his surroundings.

"Easy now. Them drunks are trouble, dontcha know. This whole night be full of them, I tell ya! They gone now."

Ben just looked up at the Good Samaritan, trying to register his words. He appreciated that anyone had come to his aid at all. He had all but given up on people and himself.

"Can you stand up?"

Ben nodded, gingerly turned over, and tried to sit up. It was excruciating, and he could not. Lenox had to do the heavy lifting, but he was no spring chicken himself. With every movement, Ben discovered a new part of him that was injured. Despite the below freezing temperatures, the throbbing pain radiated throughout his whole body.

Ironically, the pain was actually helping him regain some coherence. He delivered a sincere thanks and was met with chilling words: "Buddy, I'm sorry I didn't get to you sooner."

Buddy. It was like a whiff of smelling salts. Of the hundreds of words in the English language, to be addressed as *Buddy* had struck a nerve and given Ben some sobering perspective. "Better late than never," added Ben, who, when talking, realized how much his jaw hurt.

"Look, I got some warm coco in the lobby, and some ice. This way. Come on."

Lenox served as a physical crutch for the limping Ben as they hobbled toward The Royal Penguin Towers residential building. There, he let Ben stretch out on the red cloth sofa in a semi-enclosed waiting area while he prepared a bag of ice. There was a television set on the wall broadcasting the New Year's Eve festivities, switching between a live feed of Times Square and parties all across the world.

Ben half-heartedly watched, but mostly just stared vacantly at the Christmas tree to the left of the television set. Fond memories of his childhood seeped into his head momentarily, providing a much-needed distraction from the present. He recalled his mother and father surprising him with a few small gifts every year, nothing fancy and never the latest, hottest new toy. They did not have much growing up, but they had each other. The faint smell of roasted chestnuts and his mother's famous beef stew permeated the air. He breathed in and swore he could smell it, as though it were simmering on the stove right next to him.

He remembered sitting on his father's lap as they watched whatever football game was on. It may have been basketball, or skiing, or ice skating, for that matter. It didn't matter. The memories were vivid, but the emotions were more real than the swelling lump on his cheek, which was starting to swell and purple. It had been a simpler time in the loving confines of their home, where he never felt happier. If he had tears left to cry, they would be flowing right now.

As an adult, now without both parents, life was lonely and more difficult than he'd ever imagined. At his core, Ben was a child who enjoyed the simple things and cherished his loved ones. But the one love that had brightened his day had gone dim. The other bright light in his life has gone out. It as though he were stuck in a parallel universe vortex: *The Twilight Zone* meets *Sliding Doors*.

By the time Lenox returned with a Ziploc bag full of ice, Ben had fallen asleep.

The doorman shook his head and checked on Ben. He gently placed his palms on his icy cheeks and forehead. He checked for any areas for gushing blood or deep cuts, which was challenging through Ben's thick hair. Lenox placed the bag of ice wrapped in a thin paper towel on the cheek where Ben had absorbed a knockout punch. Ben winced for a second, then remained still. Lenox placed a festive red and white fleece blanket over Ben and whispered, "Happy New Year, buddy."

Chapter Thirty

Ida charged up to Ben and Buddy's apartment with an annoyed Kurt by her side.

"You may not want to hear this, but maybe he needs space right now. He's emotional, and if I lived in a dump like this, you better believe I'd be emotional all the freaking time," snapped Kurt as they reached the landing.

"Shoo," snapped Ida as they approached the apartment door. She knocked and then called out, "Ben?"

No response. On a whim, she turned the doorknob, and the door opened. Ida shot Kurt a concerning look, then the two slowly peeked in and announced, "Hello? Ben? It's Ida and Kurt."

They paused at the doorway, awaiting a response. But only the noisy hum of the old refrigerator greeted them.

Ida declared, "I'm coming in."

The two cautiously stepped inside. All the lights were on, and the couch had been moved, but otherwise, nothing was out of out of the ordinary—save for the numerous pills littering the kitchen floor.

Kurt noticed black latex gloves on the floor near the hallway leading to the bathroom. They looked at each other with escalating worry.

When Ida spoke, her voice was shaking. "I'm growing very worried now, Kurt."

"So am I." Kurt moved toward the counter, gingerly navigating around the pills and began examining the nearly empty bottle. He read slowly, "Benzodiazepine. What's this for?"

Ida searched her phone and after a quick read said, "Anxiety and depression, amongst other things. It's basically Xanax."

Kurt grabbed Ida's phone and began speed-reading through the pharmaceutical data, rattling off the uses, dosage, and side effects, which were nausea, diarrhea, constipation, vomiting, difficulty falling asleep or staying asleep, dry mouth, heartburn, and loss of appetite. Kurt slowed his speech. "Warning, some patients may become suicidal or have suicidal thoughts." Kurt's usual sarcastic tone dissolved into sober seriousness. "Do not take with alcohol."

Ida tried to bury her panic with logic. "If I were Ben, highly emotional, pissed off at his girlfriend, feeling guilty as sin about the negligent death of my flat mate, where would I go?"

"Those two friends of his? Deli meat guy and what's-his-face?"

"Meck and Arty?" said Ida.

"Yes, those two consolation prizes."

"It's New Year's Eve, Kurt. Meck wouldn't be caught dead at home. Arty might. Shame I have neither one's contact info."

Kurt said cautiously, "How about that Pearl person?"

Ida snickered, "What! That vermin? She's the root cause of most of this nonsense. If he went to her, he can stay there. That piece of trash…. I can't believe he would." Then her cool headedness began to crack. "Oh, this is pointless. He could be anywhere. Lying in a ditch somewhere or…"

Kurt suggested, "Hey, let's call him again. Maybe, just maybe, he'll pick up."

Full of doubt, Ida called Ben's phone again. She let it ring four times before her hope started to fade. But just before receiving the dreaded mailbox-is-full message, someone answered the phone, and it was not Ben.

A stranger's voice greeted, "Hello?"

Ida was perplexed but stammered a response. "I am trying to reach Benito Williams. With whom am I speaking?"

The man on the other line coughed and then responded, "This is Lenox Baker. Can you describe Ben, please?"

"He's just shy of six feet, gorgeous, caring, with the biggest brown eyes and a lovely nest of a hairdo." Ida had to hold her breath to keep from gushing even more.

Lenox laughed in delight. "He's had a rough night, miss, but he's resting now. I'm the doorman at The Royal Penguin Towers. Sounds like you may be just the person to cheer him up."

Ida finally exhaled before peppering him with questions. "Sir, is all right? Is he hurt? Did he mention anything about harming himself or others? Does he have a regular heartbeat? Does he know what day it is? How's his vitals?"

Kurt grabbed Ida's arm and pleaded for her to calm down.

"Ah, Well, he got roughed up by some hooligans, but he's okay now. I think he'll be fine, miss."

Ida clasped her hands over the receiver and lifted her eyes to the ceiling, looking for strength. Composed, she said, "I greatly appreciate this, sir. I shall be there in minutes. Thank you again."

Meanwhile Kurt searched for The Royal Penguin Towers on his phone and showed the display to Ida. "It's like more than half a mile from here."

A fraction of relief glazed over Ida's face. "Okay, let's go get him."

"Ida, he may need medical attention, and you have to be prepared for the fact that he may not want to see you right now."

"Well, excuse my French, but who gives a flying holy fuck! We need to go to him now! "

"I understand. I do. Trust me, I do. Which is why I will go in first, okay. Let's see what kind of shape he's in, then I'll send in the big guns." He pointed to her.

"The big guns?"

"You both are charged up emotionally, whether you believe it or not. I mean, honestly, I've never seen you like this, ever! You look like someone mother bear looking of her lost cub! Again, we don't send in the emotionally charged people first, because that's how hostages die."

"Honestly, you're an unbearable asshole sometimes!"

"I'm a correct asshole. You can't argue with me that when you are in 'Angry she-hulk mode'. And when you're like this, you are an absolutely nightmare to deal with and that's not what he needs right now."

Ida was silent but smoldering. The two were deadlocked in a staring competition before Ida gave in. "Fine. Let's just fucking go already!"

"Fine. Happy fucking New Year's Eve to me."

Chapter Thirty-one

It was nearing midnight when Ida and Kurt finally arrived at The Royal Penguin Towers. Kurt had insisted on taking a taxi, as the brutal cold was just too much for his delicate self to endure. Traffic at this hour was at a standstill, and so, after five blocks, Ida stuffed money into the driver's hand and shoved Kurt out of the vehicle. They swiftly hurried to the building, and when they got there Kurt grinded to a stop.

"So, I'll go in and see how he is, and you wait behind—"

"Will you go already!" Ida remained reluctant about Kurt's plan, but acquiesced in order to keep moving.

Inside The Royal Penguin Towers, Ida remained behind Kurt allowing him to speak to Lenox. "Good evening, sir, and Happy New Year!"

"Happy New Year to you as well," Lenox cordially replied.

"I hope you're enjoying the festivities."

"As much as I can, sir."

"I believe a very good friend of ours is here. Ben is his name."

"Yes, sir. Indeed, Ben is resting peacefully in the waiting room." Lenox turned to his side and motioned to the waiting area to his left.

Ida immediately pushed Kurt aside and rushed toward Ben, disregarding the agreed upon approach. She could not contain herself. Ida slowed as the sight of bruised and battered Ben with a Ziploc bag of ice over his head crippled her at the knees. He was still and as though in a comatose-like state. She gasped, covering her mouth and suppressing her panic. She dropped to her knees at Ben's side and cradled his head, managing to elicit only the slightest murmur.

She demanded, "Is he all right? Did he overdose? My God, was he run over by a bus?"

Lenox trailed Kurt and eased Ida. "He's okay, miss. He ran into a rough crowd. He'll be fine, but he'll be worse for wear tomorrow. The ice pack should help with the swelling. He was talking fine just before. They got him good tough. I imagine he was in no shape to be out tonight beforehand."

Ida was shocked at the man's perceptive instincts.

Kurt asked, "He didn't say anything about hurting anyone or himself?"

"Not that I can recall."

Ida doubled down. "Are you sure?"

"No, nuting like dat," said Lenox with an increasingly curious gaze.

"We're concerned he may have taken something, medication that was too strong, or something he shouldn't have."

"That, I know nuting about, sir. But if you're concerned, you best take him to the emergency room straight away."

Ida looked up at Lenox with deep sad eyes and a slight nod.

Lenox headed to his station and proceeded to call for an ambulance.

Kurt was clearly unhappy with the way this evening had gone. He had seen less of Ida these days, ever since Ben had entered her life, and this was their grand night out, something he had planned for weeks. He had stood by Ida through most of the drama between her and Spencer, but he'd never seen Ida in the delicate state she'd been in the past few hours. She had never been this emotionally open, consumed, and committed. It was eye-opening, and he knew it was all because she had never been in love like this. Ida had always been able to read her best friend without even looking at him. And it was only now that he realized he could still read her just the same. His heart went out to the two of them and was relieved that they did find Ben.

Ida rested Ben's head back onto the couch and looked up at Kurt. "What are you looking at?"

Kurt said nothing, just kissed Ida on the forehead.

Ida calmly said, "I am indebted to you for life, you know that. Not just for tonight, but for always. I've asked too much from you, and I will find some semblance of payback."

"Stop it! Besides, you don't have that kind of coin, honey."

"Listen, do me one last favor?"

Kurt raised his eyebrows in you've-got-some-nerve fashion.

"Please go to your party. I can take this from here."

"Are you serious! How can I go and leave you with this?" He demonstratively pointed both hands at the slumbering and possibly concussed Ben.

"I know you won't, and that's one of the many things I love about you. But you can also put on a good show, and you can salvage New Year's Eve for the both of us. You've already done the most amazing thing for me by bringing me here. Now go."

"Ida, no!"

She reached for and squeezed Kurt's hand. "Okay, fine. Sit in a germ-infested waiting room, and sanitize your pretty little fingers to a scratchy dry sandpaper texture as we wait all night in hospital furnishings while we watch Ben sleep."

Kurt didn't hesitate to kiss Ida on the cheek, wish her a Happy New Year and exit the lobby.

Ida returned to Ben and caressed his good cheek, awaiting an ambulance.

Chapter Thirty-two

On New Year's Day, at around 10:30 a.m., Ben was blinded by the sunshine as the drapes of his hospital room windows were opened slightly.

Nurse Kendra greeted him, "Happy New Year, sleepyhead!"

Ben was groggy, and dry-mouthed, and very much out of sorts. His head was still densely foggy, and the world spun too fast for him.

He asked in a scratchy, faint voice, "Where am I?"

"At Whitlock Medical Center," responded the nurse.

"How did I get here?"

"I brought you here," said Ida, stunning Ben. "More precisely, Kurt and I brought you here."

Ben struggled to open his eyes fully while trying to focus on Ida. His right wrist had a saline bag connected to it. She sat with a cold, unmoving demeanor, arms crossed and not smiling. Ben could not recall the events of last night coherently, but he picked up emotionally where he left off. "Why'd you bring me to here?"

"You were worked over pretty good, and unconscious due to either a concussion or an overdose or both."

"Overdose? I didn't take anything I could overdose on. I had a beer, I think."

"One beer and the benzo-Xanax thing."

Ben froze, staring up at the ceiling, trying to recall last night's events. "Oh, yeah. I couldn't open that damn bottle cap for the longest, and then it all spilled everywhere."

"So, you only had one pill?"

Ben wet his lips and corrected, "Two, I think."

"Two? Are you quite sure?"

Ben pressed his eyelids closed and nodded, "and a beer chaser."

"You should not have taken any in the first…" Ida held herself back from a full out lecture. She knew a sermon about medication responsibility would be largely ineffective at this point. She changed her course. "Nothing is more important than you in good health."

They refrained from continuing, as Nurse Kendra was finishing up her checklist. When she quietly excused herself from the room, Ben abruptly asked, "So, who's the guy?"

Ida took a breath before speaking. Kurt's warning about ditching her ramped combative approach echoed in her head. It worked well in the business world, but it would not work with Ben. She eased, "He's Spencer's brother, Eddie. Being in a thirteen-year relationship bonds family and friends. For all my formative twenties he was like an older brother to me. He was family. We're friends now, just friends. He is happily married to a gorgeous and ambitious lady, Margo, whom I adore and respect. They have the most adorable little girl, Geneva. Eddie recently got transferred to the city from Philadelphia. In those photos, we were catching up, catching up with all of them. I was showing them around town. We met precisely three times, always in public, and always platonic. It seems as though the lovely Miss Pearl is quite adept at Photoshop." She spoke the last few sentences with a grind to her teeth that felt like nails on a chalkboard.

Ben took some time digesting the new information, then asked, "Why haven't you ever mention him?"

Ida spoke with some self-righteousness. "I didn't feel compelled or obligated to. I am not the open book you are, and I should be more open. But I am not, and in this regard, I should have been. Honestly, I thought that part of my life was a distant and discontinued memory. I was resigned to never speak to or hear of them again. I feel so isolated from all that when I'm with you, like all my past, every damn sordid detail, had faded out of sight and out of mind. It's like I hit a reset button with you and..." She shifted to a more remorseful tone. "But I see now that if it will help us, I am open to telling you each and every aspect of my past. If that is all it takes to be together moving forward, then it's nothing at all."

Ben lay quiet, trying to seem indifferent. Ida couldn't tell whether he was still chemically impaired, or on the cusp of ending it all. The tension was killing her.

She added, "I left you countless messages. I'm probably the sole reason why your mailbox is full. Things happened so fast, and when I found out about the accident, I had to depart immediately."

"Accident?" asked Ben.

I da nodded then added, "Spencer has a teenager daughter. He and her mother never married, and he saw her on alternating weekends. Correction, we saw her on alternating weekend. Her name is Claudia. I grew fond of her, and I think she of me as well. In any event, in my previous life, I looked after her and spent time with her. That's something you just don't turn off as I found out yesterday, I could not as well."

205

There was silence again and the lack of feedback from Ben was unnerving. Ida kept going, "The message I received said her mother had been in a car accident, so naturally I assumed Claudia had been injured as well. I mean, why would I be contacted if her mother was injured? She and I could care less about each other. But I do care about Claudia, a great deal. When that relationship ended, I thought my place in her life was over. It hurt but I accepted it as part of life. When I feared that Claudia might in some way have sustained a life-threatening injury, I rushed to see her. Since I had no way to contact you, I left you a note. More precisely, I left the note with Pearl, the epicenter of evil."

"Note? What note?"

"Never fear, my darling. I confronted that two-faced, lying skank. She confessed to all of it and I suspect more. She said she had forgotten to show you the note. Instead, I gather, she showed you countless photos of me and my 'other life.' Her goddamn distorted private eye album! There aren't enough padded cells in the world for that one." Her quick tongue was razor sharp now, oddly arousing Ben.

She carried on, "I suppose, as they say, timing is everything, and that is precisely when you saw me exit the mysterious love limo and bid farewell to my secret family. I feel like I'm the butler from the movie *Clue*, narrating what really happened."

Ben was stunned as all the scattered pieces of that dreadful day were together forming clarity.

Ida then toned down her hyperactive diatribe and shifted into a sympathetic and serious tone. "And as cruelly ironic as this universe is, that is exactly when you found out about Buddy passing. I am so, so sorry, Ben. So deeply sorry. He was a lovely man, and a true friend. He meant so much to you and you to him."

Ben, too, suddenly lost pallor, and his eyes stop straight up into the ceiling, glazing with tears. There was too much to digest and the pain, mentally, physically and emotionally was overwhelming.

Ida moved her palm over Ben's with trepidation and held tight. She feared above all that he would immediately retract his hand, casting her out of his room and possibly out of his life. But he did not. Instead, he turned his hand over and grasped hers as tears trickled down his face.

"I'm so stupid! I am so, so stupid!"

Ida contested, "No. No. No. Nonsense. You are a beautiful man who tried to be all and do all for everyone. Some things are out of your control, and some people take advantage of that honorable part of you. Yesterday was just a really bad day."

She stood over him and turned his head toward hers, forcing eye contact. "Listen to me. I have spent most of my life largely alone, and I was fine with it. Even in a long-term relationship, I was alone. At times, I preferred it. But since meeting you, I've also learned to appreciate the company of other people—Pearl notwithstanding, or those thugs who beat you up. You have changed my life. I love you."

Ben at a loss for words. He felt grateful for her words, for her company, for her love—but he was still sorting through the pile of emotional rubble.

Ida pleaded, "Say something! Anything!"

"So, this girl, Claudia. Is she okay?"

Ida was disappointed that he had not barred his own soul but touched at his inquiry of the well-being of a child he had never met of cared for. "She's fine. She had a few bumps and bruises, not unlike yours, but she's okay. She's with Eddie but I think she has a lot of emotions to sort out."

Ben hesitated, then proposed, "Well, I guess she could stay with you until they sort things out."

Ida smiled. "That is so sweet of you to consider. But wouldn't that make for a crowded one-bedroom apartment?"

Ben smiled, and for the first time today his cheeks appeared flushed. "I'm so sorry I accused you of all that shit. I shouldn't have doubted you for a second. Pearl got the best of me, and then Buddy…"

"I thumbed through your phone while you were recovering. There's nothing to do in this dreadful place. Do you realize I've been a hospital for the better part of the last twenty-four hours? Well, these are quite clever photos. She put a lot of work into prying you from my talons. But in all seriousness, normally, you should have no reason to ever doubt me. These circumstances, however, have been extenuating, to say the least."

"I know. I can be pretty gullible. I'm sorry. I love you so much."

Ida exhaled. "You are a free and soring spirit and I adore that about you. Me, not so much, but I want to learn to be one, so I can fly along side you."

Ida had thought so much about what to say to Ben to clear everything up. She had come up with paragraphs worth of talking points about the major issues. But seeing Ben better, she basically threw all her rehearsed speeches out the window, as Ben said it best himself: "I want us to walk out of here together, come what may."

Ida nodded and gently kissed Ben on his swollen lips.

Chapter Thirty-three

Ben was discharged from the hospital later that evening after a lengthy conversation with a social worker. It was a necessary and well-meaning talk outlining the dangers of drug abuse. After reassuring the health care worker that he was fine and that this was a one-time occurrence, Ben knew he had to speak to his therapist, Dr. Hoda. He promised the social worker, Ida, Buddy's soul, and himself that he would; Ben was not in the business of empty promises. Besides, Buddy's death had left plenty weight in the land of the living.

Speaking of which, Ben knew he could no longer stay at his place, both mentally and legally. There would be too much haunting him at every corner. Before heading back to Ida's place to recover and eventually move in, Ida accompanied Ben, along with four large empty suitcases, to gather his immediate can't-live-without belongings, like his father's classic R&B LP collection, his mother's snow globe of New York City, and his own sentimental odds and ends. He had a select collection of comic books, and some special edition toys and trinkets. It was a connection he'd shared with Buddy, and to some extent with Ida—though she did gawk at the number of collectables he planned to bring. Turns out she and Ben had vastly different interpretations of what 'a few things' meant.

Needless to say, the quick trip turned into a three-hour rummage through old times. Although exhausted and emotionally spent, Ida powered through. She was genuinely happy that they, as a new couple, had endured a potentially cataclysmic, relationship-altering event. She felt the grasp of her past finally loosening it's hold. She was so comfortable with Ben, and with herself, and she was truly happy in the moment. Even the frivolity of Ben's collection brought her joy and laughter, not because of its trivialness, but because it brought Ben pure enjoyment, a childlike pleasure she secretly envied.

Each item had a story, a background of fun and irony. She learned more about Ben from his show-and-tell than she had known before. On item, Leonardo, a Teenage Mutant Ninja Turtle, was the white whale of his classic toy collection. He had lost it during a sleepover as a child and harbored its loss for decades thereafter. He finally found another one, at some small comic convention, one that he hadn't even wanted attend. Arty had talked him into going, and Ben was a miserable wet blanket until he saw a small child clutching his beloved Leonardo. Ben wasn't proud of it, but he'd distracted the child by loudly mentioning free ice cream in the food court. The kid dropped Leonardo faster than fifth period French and ran full speed toward the promise of sweets. After that, the toy was Ben's and Ben's alone.

Ida was amused. "So, there are limits to morality when it comes to doll collecting?"

"Morality is absolutely relative. And please don't call them dolls. These are *action figures.*"

They laughed, until abrupt and vehement knocking startled them. Both were genuinely scared. After all, Buddy had died here within the last forty-eight hours. Was it his spirit?

The two kept silent until the knocking started up again.

Ben motioned for Ida to stay quiet, then he asked aloud, "Who is it?"

A slurred high-pitched voice pierced their ears. "I've come to collect on our happy hour promise. You swore!"

It was Pearl. Ida's face grew angry as she mouthed in quiet contempt, "Happy Hour?"

Ben whispered, "It was purely for information. It was nothing, we were fighting. I'll explain later."

Ida was incensed, and she hissed in a loud whisper, "What else did you do promise her *purely for information?*"

"Nothing!" shouted Ben.

Pearl shouted, "What? I know you're in there, hot pants!"

Ida was smoldering. She began to roll up her sleeves and was about head for Pearl and imbed a piece of her mind into pearl's skull when Ben grabbed hold of her and said, "I love you, and I was a fool to believe her in the first place. I will handle this."

Ida was unmoved and stood with a scowl, fists still clenched. Ben stepped slowly toward the door and opened it halfway. "Pearl, what a surprise. How did you find me?"

Peal peeked in and saw no one, but she looked every bit as drunk as she sounded. She turned to Ben and batted her eyes, almost struggling to keep her eyelids open. "Your measly paychecks! They have your address on them. I bet that high-strung minx came storming after you, denying everything, huh?"

"Well, if you really must know, she—"

"She's a two-timing bitch! Can't you see that by now, you moron?" Pearl grabbed at Ben's crotch. Luckily, her coordination was two seconds slow as Ben stepped back and Pearl just caught air, and nearly fell in doing so.

Ben caught a strong whiff of her breath, which smelled like an exploded bourbon cask. "You're so wasted."

"Wasted? Nah, I'm not fucking wasted. Only thing wasted is my time!"

Pearl stumbled into the apartment and threw herself onto Ben, wrapping her free arm around him as the other arm held a half-empty bottle of whiskey. Her breath could have ignited wet wood. Ben peeled Pearl off him and pushed her back to the doorway.

He said sternly, "Pearl, you photoshopped those pics and set me up. That's not cool, *so* not cool. But not giving me that note was just as messed up."

Pearl suddenly looked shocked and outraged suddenly shouting with sober clarity. Anger can do that sometimes. "Note? What fucking note? You believe that shit-don't-stink princess whore and all the bullshit she sprinkles on you. Please. Grow up and grow a pair. Stop getting dicked by every fucking loser out there. You want a girl who is real, who you can get nasty with and who can get nasty for you. Well, she's standing right—"

"Here!" said Ida, who rounded the corner wrapped in nothing but a towel. Ben was marveled at how fast Ida had disrobed to stage this triumphant scene over Pearl. She stepped right next to Ben and groped him all over. Then she turned to Pearl. "I'm that nasty girl Ben wants. I'll get to new levels of nasty you couldn't even dream of. And I am all he will ever need. You are one pathetic piece of garbage. Go get a puppy or something. See your way out of our lives forever, or I will see to it that you're sacked and cast into the streets. I will have a word with the owner of Abbey May, Mr. Brambirch. Perhaps the New Year is the perfect time for a new staff."

Pearl was speechless as Ida sternly shoved her into the hallway. Ida reared back as though she was cocked to land a punch, but nothing happened. When Pearl opened her eyes, she found a Post-it stuck on her forehead. After the door slammed shut, Pearl removed the sticky note and read it: TRASH!

Chapter Thirty-four

Ida breathed a sigh of relief and reveled in vindication. Ben stood dumbfounded, just as shocked as Pearl had been.

Ida gathered herself, then uttered, "Okay, I think we give it ten minutes or so and we should be off. It's getting very late and we are both spent."

The taxi ride back to Ida's apartment was a relatively quiet one with a muted undercurrent of tension. They were both physically and mentally drained, and there was an uneasiness in the air, an undeniable, brooding awkwardness that was palpable. Ben thought they'd cleared everything up in the hospital, but there was a lot that happened. There were a lot of changes in the horizon. There were a lot of revelations. There were a lot of opposing emotions.

At her place, Ida sat Ben down in a dining room chair and went to get a cold pack for his cheek. She returned carrying the ice pack and a long white silk scarf. She helped him remove his denim jacket and his hooded sweatshirt, unable to keep herself from drooling over his muscular physique. Ida then used the scarf to wrap the cold pack on the side of his face. She whispered to him, "Relax, you're home now."

Ben smiled, finally feeling close to normal. Ida disappeared into the bedroom for a while. "Leave that on for about ten minutes of so. Doctors' orders!"

Ben tried hard keep the last two days out of his head but he couldn't help it. Buddy's memory crept into his heart, his passion for Ida fueled his fear of losing her and being cheated on by her. He was fatigued and sore, but also at ease.

In the bedroom, Ida had taken off her heels, her stockings and changed. She exhaled as well stopping at her mirror to recollect how far she had come in the last two days and in the least fifteen years. It was relatively easy to resolve this tipping point in their relationship. With Spencer this would have been a world war three level conflict that would have probably dissipated over time without any real resolution. They never talked things out with any depth or come to any compromise. They just butted heads like little children and held their breaths. Ben was his own man but respected enough Ida enough to hear her out completely. They moved on together instead of despite each other.

She emerged from the bedroom, tiptoeing stealthily behind Ben like a sly fox. She stroked her delicate, sensual fingers into the back of Ben's neck and began to sensually massage him. Ben welcomed the unexpected, soothing therapy.

Afterward, she slid the ice pack and scarf off Ben's cheek. He tried to turn around, but Ida steadied his head and covered his eyes with a black sleeping mask. She whispered into his ear, "This is our New Year's. Relax."

Ben suddenly felt a surge of heat that seemed to numb all his ailments. Her perfume permeated through every neural pathway like lightning bolts. The primal want was growing exponentially and doubled him over. He desperately sought to kiss her as he felt her lips leave his ear and graze his cheek. She spoke sternly, "Keep those peepers shut tight. I wouldn't want to have to take your dessert away."

He bit his swollen lip with the eagerness of an excited puppy. Every inflection of her voice deepened the ache between his legs. He was powerless, falling apart at the seams. She guided him upright and skillfully peeled off his T-shirt while still maintaining the blindfold. Then she trailed her fingers around his chest and nipples, down his abdomen, and stopped at his belt buckle. She quickly unfastened it, unbuttoned his jeans, stood him up, and shimmied his jeans and underwear off. Ben stood naked, wearing just the blindfold and was in full attention for Ida.

She gently guided him back into his seat, and again whispered seductively into his ear, "I read somewhere that sensory deprivation can enhance certain *other* senses, and I just had to find out."

Ida then straddled the chair and gently teased him by rubbing softly. She was nearly naked, save for a black lace provocative outfit. He had planned to wear this and nothing else for their New Year's Eve celebration. She thought, *Everything that needed to be said was said. This is a time for healing.*

Ida took Ben's hands and guided them up and down her body. His fingers had registered her voluptuous outline and he could not restrain himself any longer. He clasped at Ida's hips and drew her close. She resisted, flirting, "There's no rush, my dear."

Ben teased back, "Speak for yourself."

Ida placed a sleeping mask over her own eyes and replied, "Believe you me, this was weeks in the making. I can hardly wait myself."

"Oh, man! I feel like I'm being punished!" cried Ben.

"No one is being punished tonight," moaned Ida.

Chapter Thirty-five

There was no wake, no service, no funeral. As per Buddy's request, his body was buried in a VA cemetery. His will stipulated that he only wanted to be remembered for who he had been in his heyday. He wanted no tears.

Ben had to meet with a lawyer, Jacob S. Gold, Esq. The meeting had originally been scheduled for 5:30 p.m., but Ben had requested it be moved to 7:30 p.m., as he insisted Ida be there with him. He needed her, and she didn't hesitate to oblige.

The night before the meeting, Ben could not fall asleep. He lay restless for hours. The last thing he wanted to do was disturb the woman who had been his rock, so he silently slipped out of the bedroom and sat at the dining room table. He turned on his laptop but left all the other lights off. Only the glow of the screen illuminated the room. He opened his manuscript and tinkered around before slowing to a fidgeting halt. And there he remained, staring blankly for hours. He moved only to wake the computer from sleep mode.

Ida woke up sometime around 3:00 a.m. She noticed Ben wasn't by her side. The sheets were exposed and cold, the covers overturned. She wrapped herself in her fuchsia robe and staggered into the dining room to discover Ben passed out in a chair, his folded arms serving as a pillow for his head. Pity overcame her as she went to the closet retrieving a plush fleece blanket. Rather than wake him and drag him stumbling to bed, she simply laid a blanket over him and whispered, "Goodnight, my love."

Her eyes welled as she exhaled those words and returned to bed. But she lay there wide awake; it was her turn for insomnia. Her thoughts circled around Spencer and the irony of it all. Death—or near death—had a way of putting life into focus and making priorities clear. As time goes by, people forget what's important. She vowed never to.

She knew that Ben was her Now, and she wished to God that he was her Always. After their short few months together, Ben knew her more deeply than Spencer ever had in thirteen turbulent years. Ben made her laugh louder, take more risks, let her hair down all the way, and embrace life. He healed her scars and opened her eyes to becoming who she wanted to be, and he showed her that she could be and should be proud of who she was. She had learned to laugh at herself freely and break out of her shell.

"Damn!" she cursed. "As soon as you figure it all out, you might very well die!"

Spencer had been an addict from the moment she met him, and she had enabled him by not addressing it immediately. When she was with him, she drank way too much, and had partaken in other so-called recreational drugs. She'd only stayed with him out of some mechanical obligation to do so, instead of harnessing the courage to make a change.

Then there was work. She though that she was on her career path of choice, but she began to have doubts. She was meticulous, well organized and intelligent. She was articulate, sharp and commanded people's attention. Ida spoke glowingly of her superiors, most of whom she could not stand. She didn't play the game and kiss asses but she always fell in line and did not butt heads with those above her, earning her successive promotions and steady advancement. But most of her days were frustrating, and her life after work involved work. Until she met Ben, she'd been the consummate workaholic. And now, after being shown the other side of life, a real-life worth living, how could she go back?

Early that morning, Ida went out and bought some pastries before setting the coffee brewing for Ben. He was still snoring when she left for work. With all that had happened in the last few days, Ida had uncharacteristically let her e-mail inbox fill up and deadlines were fast approaching. She resolved with ironclad focus to right her ship, power through lunch, and make the attorney appointment at 7:30 p.m. tonight.

Ben finally woke up around 10:30 a.m. He was pleasantly surprised by the breakfast pastries and the love note on the bag, written in red marker: *Good morning, sunshine. Please nibble at this and know I think the world of you. Love, Ida.*

Amazing, isn't it? How the most innocuous note scribbled on a crumpled paper bag can shine a ray of happiness on an otherwise dreadful day. He managed to nibble at some pastries, which were delicious, but his appetite just wasn't there. He sipped a cup of coffee but lost interest quickly. He wandered about the apartment like a rudderless ship until entering the bedroom and collapsing onto the bed. He caught a whiff of Ida and curled under the blanket, then lay motionless until the apparitions of all his lost loved ones flooded his thoughts. Helplessly, he fell into a tearful mourn.

Just then he received a text message from Ida: *We honor our loved ones by remembering the good memories. Love you.*

The tears slowly stopped, replaced by a struggling smile. Suddenly, he remembered a second-grade class trip photo of him and his mother. It was still in his memory shoebox. Quickly, he rushed to his larger suitcase and brought out the crumbling box, which he had colored, taped, and designed over the years. It bore artwork that spanned over twenty years. Upon finding the photo, he smiled, accompanied by a glassy-eyed sigh. She had chaperoned the field trip that day. There was a patchwork of vivid memories from that trip but none other stood out like holding her hand as he skipped around. No feeling ever felt as comforting and he probably never felt as purely happy as he was on that day.

He picked up an old finger splint from when he sprained his finger in fourth grade. His mother had nursed his finger back to health, despite being weakened by dose after dose of chemotherapy.

Next, he looked at a photo of his skinny self in freshman year of high school, wearing his dad's work hat. It was oversized and greasy, but Ben looked absolutely perfect standing next to his father. He remembered wanting to one day work side by side with him.

The contents of the box sparked endless joyous memories like a New York Knicks ticket stub. Through one of his father's co-workers, he received a pair of tickets to watch the New York Knicks professional basketball team play at the famed Madison Square Arena. These tickets were far too expensive for his dad to ever afford but fate granted a childhood wish come true. Ben grew up playing basketball with his dad and he was reminded how he made him feel like a superstar, high fiving and horsing around.

Then he came across a single AK47 bullet that Buddy had given him. The bullet had Buddy's name etched in the side of it. Buddy had told him that he found it near him after getting shot at close range. His fellow soldiers killed the enemy but somehow Buddy was not shot. He found the bullet lodged in the wall behind him. He swore that by the grace of God, he was not meant to die but kept the bullet as a reminder that he was meant to live. Sadly, many of his unit did not make it out alive.

Buddy spent every day thereafter living, living hard but living free and for the most part loving and helping people. He remembered the lude jokes Buddy could crack on a dime, the wild stories he would recount from his army days, his biker gang days, and his tattoo parlor days. Buddy was a character, a friend. He gave advice when Ben didn't want it and needled into his affairs when he shouldn't have, but he always had Ben's best interest in mind. He'd made his home Ben's home.

His *thoughts* circled back to Ida, the way they always seemed to these days. She rarely spoke about her childhood, and when she did it was always regretful and brief. Her parents were successful workaholics and were emotionally and physically unavailable. Their animosity was unabashed and painfully open. As a result, Ida was often left alone, or in the care of others and vey self-conscious about appearance. Never let them see your emotions. Her sole friendly family member was her grandmother, who had passed away when Ida was in her teens. And even that relationship was not remotely as close as Ben and his parents'.

He suddenly remembered how sad her eyes became during those conversations. She had easily dealt with Buddy's passing and poorly dealt with opening up her inner most fears and deep seeded feelings. She hadn't been allowed to attend her grandmother's wake due to parental conflict. She had been hardened but was slowly softening up a spot just for Ben and perhaps for herself.

He felt for her dearly. He wanted her to be able to totally let down her barriers and feel, really feel. Today, though he needed her by his side while he grieved because she was a rock, a stone pillar. Thereafter, he wanted to make sure she was less of a rock and more of a pillow.

Later that evening, Ben arrived at Ida's office early and to her delightful surprise. He had picked up a halal takeout dinner box and black cherry seltzer, her favorite. Carmen recognized Ben, even though he seldom visited. The juicy apple of Ida's eye had brightened everyone else's days too.

When Carmen announced Ben's arrival, Ida had just finished up the last task of her day's monumental to-do list. She sparkled with glee and skipped to the door, then composed herself and allowed him in. "Why, Mr. Williams. Please, after you."

Once he entered, Ida quickly closed the door, and Carmen immediately began texting the office group chat. Before Ben could even place the food down, Ida had smothered him with a crushing embrace, which he did not mind at all. She kissed him softly, applying delicate pressure, as though he were made of crystal. It was exactly what Ben needed.

She detached and asked endearingly, "How are you holding up?"

Ben just nodded.

Ida's eyes filled with sadness, but she forced a grin.

Ben noticed and said, "I'm okay. Better actually. Your note helped a lot and your text as well. I relived some good times, and it felt damn good."

Ida's grin crested to a tearful smile as she leaped into Ben's arms. They silently held each other as time stopped.

Eventually, Ida released Ben and noticed the food by sight, and definitely by smell. "Oh, my! Have you not eaten dinner? You must be absolutely peckish!"

"Peckish? Like hungry?"

"Yes, of course."

"I am and I ain't," muttered Ben. "I picked up the combo, chicken and lamb over rice."

Ida's eyes widened as she realized her grumbling stomach. "I hadn't realized that I worked through the entire day without a meal. I might make a dreadful spectacle of myself."

Ben smiled. He said, "Please, have at it. I'm glad now that I came by so early. I didn't want to bother you."

Ida tore into the bag. "You are never a bother, and if you were, I'd let you know. Politely, of course."

Ben and his pensive quietness took a seat in a leather chair as Ida dug a spoonful of basmati rice, spicy seasoned lamb and chicken cubes, and a side of vegetables. The fried eggplant garnish was icing on the cake. Ida attacked the meal barbarically, pausing only when heartburn and hiccups set in. Then she sipped the seltzer and proclaimed, "This is food from the Gods! And you got extra hot sauce! You know me so well."

Ben nodded, still aloof. As he stared out through enormous windows at the city skyline, he asked, "So, did you get a lot done? You mentioned that you had a ton of stuff to take care of...."

She exhaled in jubilation. "Today is a day to pat myself on the back. I finished everything and then some. I must say, I even surprised myself. All the piranhas are at bay, for the time being."

He laughed. "Was there ever any doubt?"

She replied with a curt head shake and a mouthful of food.

Ben's smile faded as he again returned to the widow. Ida's appetite dwindled as her heart bled for Ben. She patted her lips clean like a lady, then walked around her desk and behind Ben's chair. She placed her hands on his shoulders and neck, massaging the tension. "Let's rub some of this away."

Ben's eyes closed as her hands magically loosened the knots, which had contorted in one tangled network. It was soothing, relaxing—and borderline painful.

Ida noted, "Let me know if I paralyze you or you can't feel a limb or something. I've never really done this before."

Ben surrendered himself and mumbled, "Keep going. It feels awesome."

After ten minutes, Ben had loosened her stiff neck tenfold. He rotated her chair and hugged her. "I love you so much."

Ida spoke softly, "And I love you more than you can ever know." Together, the two stared off into the New York skyline.

Chapter Thirty-six

The two spoke little thereafter. They decided to head to the attorney's office early to get everything over with as soon as possible. Ben wondered why he even had to go. To his knowledge, Buddy had no siblings, no children, no spouse, and no property, except whatever was in that apartment. The burial arrangements were taken care of. What else was there?

The attorney's office was on the twenty-sixth floor in one of the many skyscraping buildings in the concrete jungle. Upon entering, they were greeted by Mr. Jacob S. Gold's secretary, Mrs. Jean Beveau, who escorted Ida and Ben to a large meeting room. The office building may have been cookie-cutter, but the conference room was not. There was a long mahogany table in the center, with six chairs snugged along each side and one grand ornate chair at each end. The matching mahogany-framed chairs had high backs and black cushioned leather. The shine from the lacquer was immaculate. Soft white lights dropped from perfectly positioned modern chandeliers, which hung above each chair, creating a spotlight effect. The floor was equally as glossy as the table, but with a parquet pattern. Slate gray wallpaper with white trim molding completed the look. They spared no expense here.

Ben commented, "Okay, this room costs more than Kurt's fancy car."

Ida remained silent. Surely in her lifetime and in her industry, she had seen more extravagant rooms, but she was there to be supportive, not critique the furnishing.

Ben took a seat in the middle of the table and Ida sat right next to him. There was an eerie silence until Ben said, "I wonder—"

Then the doors opened abruptly, and two older gentlemen walked in, led by Mrs. Beveau. A portly, balding fellow in a pinstripe suit trailed behind and closed the doors.

The suit took a seat at the head of the table and rested his thick manila folder on the glossy shine. The secretary helped the two older men to chairs, nudging them into place. Across from Ben sat Mr. Devon Coleman. He was in his late seventies, dressed in a soiled mechanic jump suite that probably was older than Ben. Mr. Coleman sank in the chair and looked solemn and contemplative. Across from Ida sat Mr. Edgar Musgrove, a slight man in his sixties, but he looked older than that. He wore an off-the the-rack brown polyester suit and looked like a lifelong accountant (which he was). He fiddled with his thick eyeglasses constantly. Clearly, he never felt comfortable in the chair. As soon as everyone was squared away, Mrs. Beveau slipped out of the room unnoticed.

The spotlights had a way of making the rest of the room seem dim. The man in the suit adjusted his glasses, lowering them further and further down his nose until he could see. Then he opened his folder and flipped through the pages, scanning, reviewing, and mumbling to himself. Everyone else sat in silence, staring at the suit. Finally, he spoke without lifting his eyes from the folder, as though he were talking to the paperwork in his hands. "We're gathered here today for the reading of the last will and testament of Mr. Norbert Wilder. My secretary notarized our attendance and issued you certificates of said presence. I am Jacob Sylvester Gold, attorney at law, hired to represent Mr. Wilder's last will and testament."

Mr. Gold scanned the room slowly, purposely making eye contact with each individual. "It saddens me greatly to gather you all here under these circumstances. As such, this is the nature of our meeting. Buddy was a dear friend, a fellow infantry man and—" He wet his parched lips and paused before continuing, "A person I consider a brother. It is with a heavy heart that I execute the last of his worldly instructions. Please appreciate that I say if you here, it is because this son of a gun felt, in his heart of hearts, that you were special to him. One should never take that lightly. If you knew the man, you know that he told it like it was. I will miss that live wire like hell."

Ben and Ida were completely caught off guard, but the blend of lawyer speak and contrite familial mourning. They looked at each other and smiled. Even in death, Buddy was full of surprises.

Mr. Gold turned the page and read off a piece of thick bond paper, "To Mr. Devon Coleman, for whom I've had the pleasure of fixing bikes and cars of all sorts, I leave all the bikes I've stored at your facility over the years. I know you wanted them out of your space, but now they're staying put forever."

Mr. Coleman boomed, "That fucking asshole! Only he would leave me what I already had! I mean, shit! What a real motherfucking piece of work!"

Everyone was amused, even Mr. Gold. It was awkward to laugh at a will reading, but

Buddy would have appreciated it.

Mr. Gold continued, "Dev, only kidding. Since I can't take it with me, I leave you my riding jacket from the DMZ Hellraisers."

Mr. Coleman was clearly stunned. He had put down his wrench and power tools a long time ago. He still owned two repair shops uptown, one for bikes and one for cars. His shop had evolved into a family business, run by his trusted sons and daughters. But in biker gangs, cliques, or brotherhoods, whichever terminology you prefer, your crew was family, and your jacket was your bond. Ben turned to Ida, who looked lost, and whispered, "See, his jacket was his biker gang affiliation, his blood, his boys. It's almost as tight a bond as his army brothers. It's a huge deal."

Mr. Gold smiled with glossy eyes. He pushed his seat back and struggled to bend down. Huffing and puffing away, he eventually retrieved a box from under the table. Inside, he revealed the worn leather jacket, cracked, stiff, and discolored. Mr. Gold proudly walked over to Mr. Coleman and motioned for him to wear it.

But Mr. Coleman just stared at the jacket. Then he slowly stood up and hugged Mr. Gold. He received the jacket and examined it, finally saying, "This beat-up thing means more than you think. Back in the day, they didn't include people of color in their ranks. Sure, we could fix their bikes, but we weren't ever going to ride with em. Buddy always told me that I was his brother. And he was mine. He was some character, that Buddy, an unforgettable character."

Mr. Gold took a moment to smile. He added, "I never rode with Buddy or his crew, but I knew what that meant. It will do fine in your care, Mr. Coleman."

Then Mr. Gold cleared his throat and continued, "To Mr. Edgar Musgrove: Eddie, I leave you my entire toy collection. I know you will care for them, and not immediately put them up for sale on eBay or whatever. Use them as you like, and definitely let little David play with them. Toys are nothing if they're not played with."

Mr. Musgrove spoke eloquently, "We met decades ago at a toy collector's convention. At the time, he still rode, and they rode in the hundreds. The whole highway sounded like the inside of a muffler. I had a rarely visited table, with items most people weren't all that interested in. I was ready to give up and pack it in when this burly, broad-shouldered, heavily tattooed man in a tattered leather jacket with an unkept beard marched towards my table. He looked like a band member from ZZ Top, all coked-up. For sure, I thought I'd lose more than my wallet that day. But he scanned my table and burst into laughter. He asked how much for the whole lot. I didn't know what to say, so I commented on his bike, because, surprising for some, I used to ride. I knew a thing or two about bikes. One thing led to another and he bought most of what I had, though I refused a few of his offers on some of my most prized toys. They were out of the box and devalued, but that wasn't the point. They were my precious, rare finds. They had sentimental value to me. I'd only put them out for display. When I told him that, he eyed me pretty long, and I thought, *Here comes that killer right hook.* But instead, he bear-hugged me. He nearly broke a few ribs, but the rest is history. We would spend hours talking on the phone, about toys and comic books and bikes, which would lead into politics, the afterlife, ancient aliens, whatever his fancy. His tangent of the day."

Mr. Musgrove paused to collect himself. He took off his glasses, wiped them with a handkerchief, then opened his heart further. "He became the most unlikely, unsuspecting best friend I ever had. I've had friends that I've known longer. I had a wife for nearly thirty-five years before she passed, a seven-year-old grandson David whom I play with almost every day, but Buddy was my best friend in the whole world."

He took in a quick breath and gathered himself to finish. "When I called him a few days ago and no one picked up, I wondered. I feared. I can't tell you I knew something was wrong, but a strangeness overcame me. I do not ascribe to the supernatural readily, but later that day, I found my Ghost Rider action figure dismounted. The rider and the bike somehow fell off the shelf and onto the floor. Now I know: he was talking to me one last time."

Ida reached for Ben's hand under the table, squeezing it firm for support. She knew he felt guilty about Buddy's death. Ben's chest struggled like an accordion under water. He blinked incessantly. He felt hot, like the room was closing in on him. Under her breath, Ida said, "Breathe, it's okay. Breathe."

Mr. Gold walked over to Mr. Musgrove and bent down to hug him. They embraced for a long time and whispered words of comfort. This afforded Ben time to slow his breathing and calm himself.

Mr. Gold returned to his seat and searched for his place in the paperwork. He finally found it. "And this brings us to you, Mr. Benito Emilio Williams."

Ben looked into Mr. Gold's eyes as he read in a grave tone, "To Mr. Benito Emilio Williams, who cared for my sloppy self these last year. I entrust you with the following stipulations. First, you are in charge of my comic book collection. You are to inform Mr. Gold and his firm which five issues you choose to keep. Everything else must be donated to charities of your choosing, for life is too short to hold onto that much of anything. It is my hope that you learn that lesson. Memories are one of the most cherished parts of being human. You never gave me a reason to mistrust you, and I feared I only held you back. You and only a handful of people in my life made all the shit-swallowing worth it."

Ben thought his heart had stopped and sank to his numb toes. He slowly turned to Ida, who smiled proudly.

Mr. Gold took off his reading glasses and reclined. "You should know, from the moment you entered his life, he spoke fondly of you. He said if he'd had a son, he'd want him to be just like you. But that probably wasn't possible, because of his 'screwy, fucked-up genes'."

Mr. Gold ended his speech with a cheerful smile. Then Mr. Musgrove added, "He was always wondering, 'What's this great kid doing with a bum like me! He should be chasing skirts, getting high.

Get him a bike, why dontcha!' But I saw through that. I knew he was lucky to have you. And I know you were lucky too."

Ben drew in a deep breath that seemed to have no exhale. From beyond the grave, Buddy had entrusted him with a mission. The flattery from all the strangers was hard to digest. For all that he did for Buddy, Ben always felt like he could have done more. He could have at the very least been by his side during his last moments. Instead, Buddy died alone, probably gasping, clawing. And here, these close friends of Buddy's thought so highly of him. They didn't know his pain, or that Ben felt like a fraud.

The testimonials echoed like an unrelenting migraine, and then Ben snapped, "I'm sorry, but you must know. I was not with Buddy the night he passed. I wasn't home the night before that either. Truthfully, I wasn't home too often the past few months. Heck, many nights, many weekends, I wasn't there. I didn't even call. At the very least, I shoulda called or stopped by to check on him more often. Maybe I could have called nine-one-one or something. I'm not some great guy! I'm sorry. I'm not."

Uncertain silence filled the room. The uneasiness was heavy. Ida was at a loss for words and kept her eyes lowered. She had been settling into elation with Ben, and now shared a similar shame and guilt. Their time together had directly taken time from Ben and Buddy.

Mr. Musgrove broke in with a cracked, yet soothing voice, "Son, look, you have every right to spend time with this beautiful young lady. Every gosh darn right! You are young and in love. A blind man can see that. Buddy lived three lifetimes, maybe more, and he was not cheated one cent in this life. He always told me after his tour he go a second lease on life." Mr. Musgrove paused. "He called you an angel, a godsend, and you know as well as I do that he never minced words or lied about anything. You did plenty right by him, maybe more than plenty. You, me, or anyone else can't be at everyone's side all the time. We all have to live and love and die. This is life and he wasn't alone."

Mr. Coleman added, "Everyone dies, young fella. It's how you live that matters. Always remember that." With that, he slowly rose, gathered the leather jacket, and made his rounds, hugging, shaking hands, and exchanging words of serenity and hope.

Mr. Musgrove followed suit. Then Mr. Gold addressed Ben and Ida. "I can't sum up more eloquently than that. I'm more toward the end of the line than the beginning, but I can tell you: truer words were never spoken. It was Buddy's time. One day, it will be mine, and then yours. Go out there and seize the day, then come home and sleep in peace. Come what may."

Chapter Thirty-seven

In the neighborhood of one and a half years later, Ben was just about done setting up his display. He was at the Small Press Expo in Bethesda, Maryland. The Small Press Expo, or SPX, was created in 1994 to promote artists and publishers who produce independent comics. The event hosts an annual festival that provides a forum for artists, writers, and publishers of comic art in all its various forms. Its goal is to present to the public comic art not accessible through traditional commercial channels. No major big business retailers are allowed at the convention, so even the small-time beginners have a shot to show their stuff.

Ben was a rising star, and he impressed all who passed by. His table was dressed in a black velvet tablecloth with red tassel. It was littered with pins, bookmarks, and a signup sheet for e-mails. To his right, stacked on a transparent display case, was his heralded novel, *The Sunrise Apocalypse*. To his left was a prototype first draft graphic novel of the same name. Behind his first novel was a poster display for *Wrath of the Shadow Queen*, the sequel.

Behind him was an eight-foot-tall banner, complete with flashing LED lights. Arty had crafted the banner himself, and it helped Ben stand out from his fellow presenters. Arty was circulating the venue as well, speaking to other artists, self-publishers, and people in general. Turns out the banner had rekindled the spark in his dormant brush and easel.

Ben's first novel was not an instant success, but it was slowly gaining traction. This was largely due Ida's support—she had tons of advertising connections. The right people at the right time had made a world of difference. She knew a person who knew an agent, who knew an editor, who knew everyone else.

Ida herself had since moved on from her medical sales firm. She'd been blown away by Ben's manuscript and labored tirelessly to market his work. In doing so she became intrigued by the world of publishing, especially the print-on-demand possibilities and the plight of independent authors. The money was a fraction of her former position, but this industry was exponentially more rewarding and infinitely more exciting. She stayed on as a corporate consultant with her old job but had to give up the apartment. The two moved into a quaint little one bedroom in Queens. The new neighborhood had a more diverse culture and was richly vibrant with artists and musicians.

After he self-published his book, days at a time went by without a sale. Ida and all of his friends had sworn, on Ben's insistence, not to be the first buyer. The first sale had to be a real sale, from a real stranger with a genuine interest. By day three that very first sale was made, and nothing compared to that euphoric moment. The couple celebrated as only they could, with joy, take-out and passion. By the end of the week more than a hundred people had bought it. By the end of the month, he had over a thousand sales. By the three-month marker, agents had taken notice and started to contact Ben.

Ben had taken Ida's suggestion to heart and visited some of his and Arty's artist friends to work on a graphic novel version of his book. It took some tweaking and discussion, but it finally his words were finally realized into illustrated life. For Ida and Ben, holding

Issue #1 of *Saga* side by side with Issue #1 of *The Sunrise apocalypse* was as surreal and exhilarating as it gets.

Ben could not have been more appreciative for what Ida had done for him. Beyond the tangibles of the laptop, the start-up funding, the overhead costs, the rent-free living, and the business connections, she had jolted him to the finish line by insisting Ben take a few months off from work and finish the book. She had provided him with calmness, support, and an honest, critical eye. She filled a void in him, one that had needed someone to trust, to love, and to inspire. She had done that, and so much more. They had healed each other, had allowed for a safe place to share fears, anxieties, and insecurities. Together, obstacles in life seemed easier and didn't feel so unconquerable. There was an inner peace in finding that white whale called true love.

Back at SPX, Ben was holding his own, engaging large groups without ever neglecting anyone, no matter how many times he had to relay the same spiel. As he spoke, more and more people gathered.

"Thank you all again for stopping at my table and checking out the book and the video and the upcoming projects. Kindly leave your contact info on our mailing list. Today only buy *The Sunrise Apocalypse* and get fifty percent off the limited issue release of its sequel, *Wrath of the Shadow Queen.*

One patron asked, "When is the sequel coming out as on digital?"

Ida fielded this question, "*The Sunrise Apocalypse is already available as an e-book*, the *Wrath of the Shadow Queen* debuts in two weeks. So in the meantime get your signed copy by Benito Williams himself today for the ridiculously bargain price.

He and Ida looked at each other sharing the singular giddiness as children at a lemonade stand tending to a crowd of enthusiast. Ben brimmed with appreciation still unable to fully comprehend the level of success he is enjoying.

Another patron asked, "What was your inspiration for this crazy world you built in the sci-fi romance fantasy sage?"

Ben paused and again looked over at Ida. Ida shared the same curiosity as the patron. He then answered, "We don't ever know where we're going, but we all know where we've been and what breaks us may build us, but we do leave something behind. I guess, in my world vision, the two central characters find what they've left behind in each other and then some. I just had to make it a hundred times more bat-shit crazy!"

"Dude, you must have tripped out on some wicked shit to meld a space seed zombie virus with mutated metallic based aliens and the formless demigods who designed all of this. Yo, then then you killed them off and destroy the cure with them. Freakin bananas, bro!"

Ben smiled ear to ear, "You think that's nuts, check out the whole min-world within that world in the sequel!"

He could almost hear Ida's thoughts of *well-played.* Her mastery manipulation of eager buyers had taught him a thing or two. The crowd clamored for more as Ben and Ida were suddenly drowned in a barrage of indecipherable questions.

Ida reached for a remote and pressed play. All of a sudden, the large screen behind him came to life,. She announced, "Everyone, if you would all kindly direct your attention to the screen, we have a short presentation of the soon to be released graphic novel version of *The Sunrise Apocalypse.*" A hush had quelled the immediate patrons as well as fringe on-lookers. Even more people gathered around the table. She nodded to Ben. Meck had shaken off his video-editing cobwebs and produced a spectacular, polished book trailer for Ben. Like Arty, the project had helped Meck reboot his own interest in the audiovisual arts.

The opening scene showed an alien autopsy where mechanical arms dig in deep with brutal disregard to retrieve a glowing capsule.

Panning backwards revealed an assortment of alien lifeforms and a few scattered humans. Once the item was harvested, one alien, a hybrid reptile-cyborg opened the device. A witch-like creature emerged and in graphic violent fashion dispatched all the participants ending with the cryptic words of, "Revenge will be mine!"

The audience erupted in elation and wanted more.

As Ida re-engaged the crowd, Ben grabbed a book and began writing in the front cover. In particular, an older gentleman dressed in full businessman attire approached and stood out from most of the casual attendees. He spoke to Ida briefly, who then led him toward Ben. "Ben, this is Bogart Jimenez, from Savage Heart Publishing. He'd like a word with you."

Ben could not keep up with all these doors opening at once. Before he slipped away to speak to Mr. Jimenez in more detail, he placed the book in Ida's hand and motioned for her to read it. Then Ben and Mr. Jimenez escaped the melee of his floorspace finding a quieter spot—as if there were such a thing.

As Ida watched Ben walk off, she cracked open the book and read as quickly as she could. The captivating video presentation was nearing the end, and Ida anticipated loads of questions. Ben's book jacket inscription read: *I want you by my side forever, come what may. I want to wake up next to you every day of my life! No one fits like you. Will you marry me? Love, Ben.*

She cursed him lovingly as she held back the tears. She could not have been prouder.

Ben was staring wide-eyed at the businessman. Mr. Jimenez had his undivided ear, and Ben was overwhelmed by his kind words about his story. Mr. Jimenez had a salesman's charm but subtle undertone of childlike amazement, a quality very hard to fake.

Mr. Jimenez got to the point, "So what I was saying is that I've been tracking your independent success and am remarkably impressed. I mean just look over at your table and everyone else's. You got it. We want to have a more formal conversation about coming on board with Savage Heart Publishing. Together I think we can do great things."

Ben was absolutely floored only mustering, "Wow."

Mr. Jimenez held up his hand holding Ben's attention as he took out his phone and then after a few finger swipes, showed Ben some of their latest clients and their works, "See here are a few of the latest talents to come aboard. These are their sales before and after signing on."

Ben's eyes nearly popped out of their sockets. "Holy shit! That's insane!"

Mr. Jimenez laughed and said, "You've achieved outstanding success, all by yourself. With our connections and marketing team, we project you'll blow this rocket ship to a whole other stratosphere!"

Ben wore a glazed look of disbelief. His heart was beating as if he'd just won the jackpot. He tried to keep grounded reminding himself about all the fluff agents float out there. But he recognized a few names, and the figures were staggering.

Mr. Jimenez continued, "I know you're supremely talented, and you surely will receive many more offers, but please strongly consider us. Oh, and by the way, we do have a line of graphic novels as well. We can partner with your illustrators and work something out. Let's leave this as an open conversation." Mr. Jimenez handed Ben his card and firmly shook his hand. "We look forward to speaking with you very soon."

As Mr. Jimenez left, smiling and hopeful, Ben slowly meandered back toward his table, numbed with shellshock.

Ida had been handing out business cards and promo items and handed off the sales to Arty. Ida hurried towards Ben with the book he gave her in hand, intercepting him before he returned to the madness of his table. They were afforded a rare few seconds alone.

Chapter Thirty-seven

Ida sked, "So?"

Ben attempted many times to articulate his thoughts before resolving, "You know all this doesn't happen without you, right? I mean not the sales, the video, the sequel, this guy. I mean..." Ben took hold of Ida's hand and held it tight to his chest. "All of it and all of you, of us! This is you and I together."

Ida smiled as wide as her lips can stretch. As a person, she had traveled a lifetime since meeting Ben, career-wise and emotionally. She had found a happiness in herself that she had never known existed. She held in the excitement of a million supernovas but could not contain it any longer. Her intense brown eyes were glazed and piercing into Ben's. She cracked open the book to the Ben's inscription and let him read her response aloud: *I do.*

THE END,

BUT REALLY, ITS JUST THE BEGINGING